The six horses came running out of the barn, with Lennon and Hall looking for Clint to be astride one of them. Because of that they did not see Clint running behind the horses until too late. They were out in the open when he fired, hitting Hall with his first shot. By the time Lennon realized what was going on it was too late. He tried to bring his gun to bear on Clint, but there just wasn't time. Clint fired and his bullet struck Vic Lennon in the chest. Lennon went to his knees, his gun pointed to the ground . . .

DON'T MISS THESE
ALL-ACTION WESTERN SERIES
FROM THE BERKLEY PUBLISHING GROUP

THE GUNSMITH by J. R. Roberts
Clint Adams was a legend among lawmen, outlaws, and ladies. They called him . . . the Gunsmith.

LONGARM by Tabor Evans
The popular long-running series about U.S. Deputy Marshal Long—his life, his loves, his fight for justice.

SLOCUM by Jake Logan
Today's longest-running action Western. John Slocum rides a deadly trail of hot blood and cold steel.

McMASTERS by Lee Morgan
The blazing new series from the creators of *Longarm*. When McMasters shoots, he shoots to kill. To his enemies, he is the most dangerous man they have ever known.

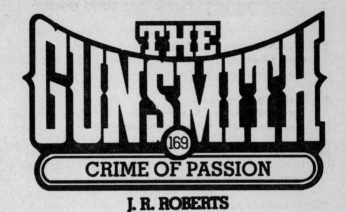

THE GUNSMITH

169

CRIME OF PASSION

J. R. ROBERTS

JOVE BOOKS, NEW YORK

CRIME OF PASSION

A Jove Book / published by arrangement with
the author

PRINTING HISTORY
Jove edition / January 1996

All rights reserved.
Copyright © 1996 by Robert J. Randisi.
This book may not be reproduced in whole
or in part, by mimeograph or any other means,
without permission. For information address:
The Berkley Publishing Group, 200 Madison Avenue,
New York, New York 10016.

ISBN: 0-515-11784-6

A JOVE BOOK®
Jove Books are published by The Berkley Publishing Group,
200 Madison Avenue, New York, New York 10016.
JOVE and the "J" design are trademarks
belonging to Jove Publications, Inc.

PRINTED IN THE UNITED STATES OF AMERICA

10 9 8 7 6 5 4 3 2 1

PROLOGUE

Lawrence Dain loved guns. He couldn't shoot very well, but he enjoyed owning them and keeping them on display. On his ranch outside of Rogue's Walk, Montana, in his home, he had an entire room devoted to them. At fifty-five years of age Lawrence Dain was wealthy enough to devote entire homes to his whims if he so desired. However, he was satisfied with owning this one, and dedicating this room to his gun collection.

On this particular morning he was enjoying an eighteenth-century Snaphaunce, turning it over and over in his hand, when his wife came to the door of the room, ostensibly called the den for want of another word.

"Lawrence?"

"Hmm?"

She was used to this. When he was engrossed in

his guns, he often didn't hear her or pay attention to her. At thirty-five Gloria Dain was twenty years younger than her husband. They were married three years, and she was his second wife.

"Lawrence?" she said again, louder.

He turned this time but gave her only a cursory look before turning his attention back to the gun in his hand. He placed it back in its glass case and then turned to give her his full attention.

"What is it, my dear?"

"Henry is here."

Henry Bollinger was Dain's lawyer and longtime friend.

"Well, bring him in, darling," he said. "Don't keep him waiting."

Gloria knew that if she had brought Henry with her to the den she would have paid the price later— a vicious tongue-lashing—for interrupting her husband without first announcing Bollinger's presence.

"Yes, dear."

Dain turned his attention back to his collection and was busily admiring a Colt that had been personally constructed for him by Sam Colt when Henry Bollinger entered the room.

"Lawrence?"

"Beautiful, isn't it?" Dain asked. "This was made specifically for me."

"Yes," Bollinger said, "I know, Lawrence."

"Hmm?" Dain looked at his friend. "Oh, yes, of course you do."

Bollinger waited while Dain lovingly placed the weapon back in its case.

"Brandy?" Dain offered.

"Yes, thanks."

Dain poured two snifters of brandy and handed one to Bollinger. The two men then sat across from each other, one in each love seat. The house had been decorated by Dain's first wife, Patrice, and he had not allowed Gloria to change a stick of furniture.

"Have you found him?" Dain asked.

"Yes, I believe I have," Bollinger said. "He uses a South Texas town called Labyrinth as a sort of unofficial base. Now, most of the year he is out traveling, but I believe he is there now."

"Then go and talk to him."

Bollinger stared at Dain.

"Me?" he asked. "You want me to talk to him?"

"You're my lawyer, aren't you, Henry?"

"Well, yes . . ."

"You handle my business affairs?"

"Yes, I do, but—"

"Consider this business, then," Dain said. "Go and talk to him."

"But . . . he's the Gunsmith."

Bollinger had lowered his voice, as if afraid someone would overhear.

"I know who he is, Henry," Dain said. "That's why I want you to go and talk to him."

"But—"

"He's not going to bite you."

"I know, but—"

"Then it's settled."

"It isn't—"

"You'll go," Dain said with finality, "and that's that."

"This might be expensive, Lawrence," Bollinger said, trying a different tack.

"I don't care how expensive it is, Henry," Dain said. "I want this. It would be the jewel in the crown of my collection."

"And if he doesn't agree?"

"Why wouldn't he?" Dain said. "Just tell him it's for me."

"What if that doesn't—"

"Who is the foremost gun collector in the country, Henry?"

"You are."

"In the world?"

"Probably you."

"Then why would he refuse?"

"I don't know," Bollinger said after a moment of helpless silence. "I'm just playing devil's advocate."

"Well, don't," Lawrence Dain said. "Just get your ass out of my chair, out of my house, and go and see him."

"Yes, well—"

"Now."

Bollinger sat forward and looked for a place to set down his glass of untouched brandy. Dain reached out and took it from him.

"Go," he said.

Bollinger stood up and hurried from the room.

Gloria Dain was waiting for him in the entry foyer. As always her beauty took his breath away. She was a statuesque, dark-haired beauty with flawless skin. Bollinger could not fathom how this woman could be relegated to second position in Lawrence Dain's life, behind his gun collection. Then again, Henry Bollinger had never collected anything in his life.

"Why do you let him talk to you that way, Henry?" she asked.

"Gloria, you don't understand—"

"I understand that you are smarter than he is," Gloria said. "I understand that he would not be as wealthy as he is without you."

"Well—"

"And he knows it, too," she said. "That's why he treats you this way."

"Gloria—"

"Now you're supposed to go running off to Texas to see some common gunman—"

"Clint Adams is not a common gunman, Gloria—"

Gloria Dain cut Bollinger off with a look and a shake of her head. Oh, what he wouldn't give to have her look at him differently. But how could she? He was short, heavy, balding, and he worked for her husband.

"I have to go, Gloria."

"Go ahead, then," she said. "Do your master's bidding. He wastes so much money on those damned guns!"

Her last words were spoken with frustration. He wished he could change things for her, but he couldn't. She was stuck in a loveless marriage with a man who had taken her out of a saloon and made her an ornament for his arm. Henry Bollinger was just not man enough to change her life for her.

By God, he couldn't even change his own.

Gloria Dain knew that her husband was sending Henry Bollinger off to spend some obscene amount of money on yet another gun. She did not understand her husband's passion to collect guns—many of which did not even fire. What was the point?

Because she knew her husband would be in the den for hours, fondling his collection, Gloria slipped from the house and went to find Del Nolan, the foreman of the ranch. At least Nolan knew which needed more fondling, a woman or a gun.

ONE

Clint was awakened by the insistent pounding on his hotel room door. He turned over and reached out his arm, encountering only empty bed sheets. Then he remembered that Priscilla, the woman who had come back to the room with him the night before, had awakened at six A.M., insisted on his attentions, and then had departed at seven, after which he fell right back to sleep. He didn't know where the woman got her energy. Was that her at the door now, coming back for still more? Maybe, he thought, if he ignored her she'd go away.

Priscilla Wentworth was a hard woman to ignore, though. Tall, willowy except for an impressive bosom, she had pale skin that was as smooth as marble. Once the thought of her invaded his mind there was no way he could ignore her.

"I'm coming, I'm coming," he called out, swinging

his feet to the floor. He started to reach for a pair of pants, but then realized that she had already seen him as naked as he could get. He stood up, walked to the door, and opened it.

It was not Priscilla.

It was Harvey, the desk clerk, a portly, balding man who was now studiously avoiding looking anywhere but right into Clint Adams's eyes.

"What time is it, Harvey?"

"It's about ten, Mr. Adams."

"That late?" The early morning session with Priscilla must have worn him out more than he'd thought. He rarely—if ever—slept this late.

"Sorry to wake you, Mr. Adams, but—"

"That's okay, Harvey," Clint said, backing away from the door, "it's too late to be sleeping, anyway."

Clint grabbed his pants and pulled them on, thereby making himself and Harvey a little less uncomfortable with each other.

"What can I do for you, Harvey?"

"Mr. Hartman sent over word that I was to wake you, Mr. Adams."

"He did, huh? Why?"

"He says you should get over to his place as soon as you can."

"Did he say why?"

"No, sir. The only message I got was that you was supposed to come. Oh, yeah, there was somethin' about somebody wantin' to see you, but I don't know who."

"All right, Harvey," Clint said, "send word to Mr.

Hartman that I'll be over there just as soon as I get dressed."

"Yes, sir," Harvey said, "I'll do that, Mr. Adams."

As Harvey closed the door, Clint wondered what was so important that Rick had to send a messenger over to have him woken up. Well, there was only one way to find out. He took off his pants so that he'd be able to put on a pair of underwear, and then the pants again. A quick wash and he donned his shirt, socks, and boots, then strapped on his gun. He thought that at the very least Hartman had better have coffee ready.

TWO

When Clint reached Rick's Place, Rick Hartman did indeed have coffee waiting. He also had breakfast on the table, and was sitting with a man Clint had never seen before.

"Ah, here's Clint now," Hartman said, standing as Clint entered.

The man looked at Clint and then also stood. He was well dressed, wearing a suit Clint was sure had cost more than everything he owned at the moment. He was in his forties, not an attractive man, which was probably why he wore such expensive clothes. He wore wire-framed glasses, from behind which stared two watery blue eyes.

"This better be good, Rick," Clint said as Hartman approached him.

"You're gonna like this a lot, Clint," Hartman assured him in a low voice. "Just be civil and let the man introduce himself."

"When I get some coffee in me," Clint said, "I'll be civil."

"There's plenty of coffee," Hartman said, leading Clint to the table. "Clint Adams, meet Henry Bollinger," Rick Hartman said.

"It's a pleasure to meet you, Mr. Adams," Bollinger said, putting out his hand.

Clint took the man's hand and released it as soon as possible. He never understood why men with limp, wet handshakes even bothered with the formality.

"Mr. Bollinger," Clint said curtly. He was eyeing the coffeepot on the table.

"Why don't we sit down and I'll have more breakfast brought out," Hartman suggested, then hastily added, "and more coffee."

Clint sat down opposite Henry Bollinger and poured himself a cup of coffee.

"Clint," Hartman said, "Mr. Bollinger represents Lawrence Dain."

Clint stopped pouring, put the coffeepot down, and looked at Henry Bollinger with interest. Lawrence Dain was only the possessor of one of the country's—and maybe the world's—three most valuable gun collections.

"Is Mr. Dain in town?" Clint asked.

"No, I'm afraid he is not," Bollinger answered. "As Mr. Hartman said, I am representing him." Bollinger waited a moment before adding, as an afterthought, "I am his attorney."

"I see," Clint said.

Breakfast was brought to the table then by two of

the girls who worked for Hartman. Their usual job was not waiting tables, but they managed to serve the meals without spilling anything. Lane, the blonde, grinned at Clint and made a face when she was sure neither Hartman nor Bollinger could see her. Clint held back a laugh.

"Well, then, Mr. Bollinger," Clint said, when the women had left, "maybe you've already told Mr. Hartman, but I'd certainly like to know why you're in Labyrinth, and what it has to do with me."

"It has everything to do with you, sir," Bollinger said. "I am, after all, here specifically to see you."

Clint's heart quickened, but he was careful not to show it.

"Well, maybe you'll tell me what it is I can do for you, Mr. Bollinger . . . or for Mr. Dain."

"Mr. Dain has sent me here to try to convince you to build a weapon for him." Bollinger cleared his throat and added, "That is, a gun."

"Well, I'm flattered," Clint said.

"Mr. Dain considers you one of the premier, uh, gunsmiths in the country, Mr. Adams . . . perhaps even the world."

Clint doubted that. It was more likely Mr. Dain simply wanted a gun in his collection that was crafted not by *a* gunsmith but by *the* Gunsmith.

Still, to have a gun in the man's collection . . .

"That's very kind of him."

"He has sent me to negotiate a price . . . that is, if you agree to, uh, perform the service."

"I see."

"So if you will tell me how much you will require—"

Bollinger continued, but Clint held up his hand to stop the man.

"Just a minute, Mr. Bollinger," he said. "I haven't said that I will do it."

"I'm sorry?" Bollinger said, looking puzzled.

"Clint—" Hartman started, but stopped when Clint looked at him.

"Mr. Adams," Bollinger said, "surely you know who Mr. Dain is?"

"I'm very well acquainted with Mr. Dain's reputation, Mr. Bollinger."

"Then . . . why would you refuse this commission?"

"I haven't refused it."

"But . . ."

"I would simply like to think it over."

"But Mr. Dain will pay you—"

"I'd like to think it over even before an offer is proposed, Mr. Bollinger. You're an attorney, a businessman. Surely you can understand that?"

It was plain that Bollinger couldn't understand it, but he would never have said so.

"Well, yes, uh, of course—"

"Good," Clint said, "then why don't we eat our breakfast, and we can discuss the matter later. Rick?"

"Huh?" Hartman said, obviously also confused.

"Didn't you say something about fresh coffee?"

THREE

After breakfast Bollinger said he had to go and send a telegram.

"To your boss?" Hartman asked.

Bollinger nodded.

"I have to inform him of my progress," Bollinger said, with a last glance at Clint, who said nothing. "Well . . . we can talk later," he finally said.

"Yes, let's do that," Clint said. "At dinner?"

"Here?"

"At your hotel," Clint said. There were two hotels in town. Clint didn't know which one the man was staying at, but it didn't matter. Each had their own dining room.

"Very well," Bollinger said, and he left.

"What the hell are you thinkin' about?" Hartman exploded when Bollinger was gone.

Clint poured himself another cup of coffee.

"This is Lawrence Dain we're talkin' about here,"

Hartman continued. "Do you know what it would mean to you to have a gun in his collection?"

Clint looked at his friend.

"I'm thinking about what it would mean to him to have a gun built by me in his collection."

Hartman stared at Clint for a few moments, then leaned back.

"You're drivin' the price up."

"Let's just say I'm not taking the offer at face value."

"Why not?"

"Why didn't Dain come himself?"

"Dain is a wealthy man, Clint," Hartman said. "They very rarely carry their own messages."

"This is not a message, this is a business offer," Clint said.

Hartman waved a hand and said, "Same thing. To rich people it's all the same thing."

Clint rubbed his jaw and said, "Maybe."

"Just drive the price up and go ahead and accept," Hartman said. "You been sittin' around here for weeks bellyachin' about not havin' anythin' to do. This is better than jumping on Duke's back and goin' off with no direction in mind. Every time you do that you end up gettin' in trouble."

Hartman had a point there.

"Don't be so suspicious, Clint," Hartman went on. "Just take the job."

Clint looked at Hartman and said, "It is sort of flattering."

"Sort of?"

"Well . . . that is, unless he just wants to have a gun

in his collection built by the Gunsmith."

Hartman sat forward and said, "Wake up, man! That's what he wants, and what's wrong with that? Clint Adams, the Gunsmith? They're one and the same."

"I guess so."

"Clint," Hartman said, "Dain has a gun built for him by Sam Colt himself."

"Hmm," Clint said. That was good company, for sure.

"Why don't you try to catch him before he sends his telegram?"

Clint thought a moment.

"No, you were right the first time."

"About what?"

"About running the price up," Clint said. "If I'm going to do this it's going to be expensive."

"How? You have your equipment."

"My equipment?" Clint said derisively. "That's only good for easy repairs. No, for something like this I'm going to need the best equipment I can get my hands on."

"And you'll buy it?"

"Maybe," Clint said, "or maybe . . ."

"Maybe what?" Hartman asked, after a moment.

"Maybe I can borrow it."

"From who?"

Instead of answering Clint got up and started out.

"Hey! Where are you going?"

"To send a telegram of my own."

FOUR

Clint waited across the street from the telegraph office until Bollinger finished his business and left. When the man was out of sight, he crossed and entered the office. The clerk, William, knew him on sight.

"Hello, Mr. Adams."

"William."

"Got a telegram to send?"

"Yes, I do."

He pulled over a slip of paper and picked up a pencil. He wrote a short note asking for a favor and then handed it over to William.

"You're gonna do it, then?" William asked.

"Do what?"

William looked sheepish. He was a small man, barely five five, and probably didn't weigh more than one hundred and twenty pounds.

"I couldn't help—I mean, I have to read them

17

when I send them, don't I?"

"I suppose so."

"So I couldn't help finding out that Lawrence Dain wants to commission you to build a gun for him."

"Uh-huh. What else did you find out?"

"Well . . . you don't seem too anxious to accept."

"Is that what Mr. Bollinger's telegram said?"

"Well, I can't really tell you—"

"William."

. William made a show of looking around before answering.

"All it said was that he was negotiating with you."

"And from that you assumed I wasn't too anxious to take the job?"

"Either that or you're tryin' to drive the price up."

"And now from my telegram you assume I am going to take the job?"

William stared at Clint for a few moments, then averted his eyes.

"I guess maybe I better just send it."

"I guess maybe you better."

After William sent Clint's telegram, Clint said, "Find me with the answer as soon as it comes in."

"Sure, Mr. Adams."

Clint started out, then turned back.

"William?"

"Yeah?"

"Was Mr. Bollinger expecting a reply?"

"No," William said. "Not that he mentioned."

"Did he say where he was staying?"

"The other hotel."

That meant he wasn't staying in the same hotel as

Clint, the Labyrinth House.

"Okay, thanks."

"I'll get the reply to you as soon as it comes in."

"Thanks."

Clint's telegram had been sent to a man named Mick Bolton, possibly the finest gunsmith Clint knew. Bolton lived in New Mexico and had every gunsmithing tool imaginable. If Clint decided to accept Dain's commission, he hoped that Bolton would let him come and use his workshop.

The reply came in several hours later, while Clint was sitting in front of his hotel.

"Thanks, William."

"You gonna do it?" William asked.

Clint just stared at him, and William backed away and went back to his office.

Clint read the reply, which said simply: COME AHEAD.

He folded the telegram, put it in his pocket, and waited for Bollinger to show up.

FIVE

Clint wasn't surprised when Rick Hartman showed up.

"I was in at the start," Hartman said. "I figured you wouldn't mind."

"I never did hear *how* you got into it from the start," Clint said. "Why did Bollinger find you before me?"

"He came into my place the night before for a drink," Hartman said. "He asked the bartender about you, and he put him onto me."

"Where was I?"

"Well," Hartman said, "if I remember correctly, you were a little busy in your hotel room."

Clint glared at him.

"Well, after all," Hartman said, "I did give Priscilla the rest of the night off, didn't I?"

He was about to reply when Bollinger appeared across the street and started toward them. Clint stood up next to Hartman, who had already been standing.

"Mr. Adams," Bollinger said. He looked at Hartman, obviously puzzled by his presence.

"I asked Mr. Hartman to have dinner with us, Mr. Bollinger," Clint said. "I hope you don't mind."

"Oh . . . no, not at all."

"Let's go in, then," Clint said.

"Yes, by all means," Bollinger said, "let's."

Over dinner Clint and Bollinger talked price while Hartman listened in silence.

"Just how anxious is Mr. Dain to have a gun built by me in his collection?" Clint asked.

"Well . . . he's very anxious."

"Then he should be willing to pay, right?"

"He is, but . . ."

"I'll have to use the best tools, you know."

"Well—"

"And I don't have them here."

Bollinger hesitated, then said, "I see. You'll be wanting to buy that equipment, then?"

"I don't know yet," Clint said, "but I want to know what options I have open to me. Will Mr. Dain be paying all expenses?"

"Yes," Bollinger said, then added, "within reason. You'll be supplying receipts, of course."

"Of course."

"Then I think we can safely say that your expenses will be covered."

"Then all that needs to be settled is the main price for the gun," Clint said.

"And the kind of gun?" Hartman asked.

Clint looked at his friend and said, "Good point, Rick." He turned his attention back to Bollinger. "I assume we're talking about a pistol."

"Yes," Bollinger said, "Mr. Dain's entire collection is comprised of handguns."

"Good," Clint said. He preferred to work with pistols rather than rifles or anything fancy. "How much is Mr. Dain proposing to pay?"

Bollinger named a figure that made Hartman sit back. Clint, however, didn't flinch.

"Are you empowered to do all negotiating, Mr. Bollinger?" Clint asked. "Or do you have to check with your employer?"

"I have the honor of my employer's confidence," Bollinger said. "I can negotiate."

"Good," Clint said, "then let's do it."

An hour later they were having coffee.

"You drive a hard bargain, Mr. Adams," Bollinger said.

Clint had the feeling that Bollinger was more surprised than impressed.

"So do you, Mr. Bollinger," Clint said. "I can see why you have Mr. Dain's confidence."

Bollinger stood up and signaled for a waiter. He settled the bill, paying for all three dinners.

"I'll send a telegram to Mr. Dain telling him that all the arrangements have been made," he said. "He'll be very pleased."

"I hope so," Clint said.

"The only thing we haven't discussed is a delivery date," the lawyer said.

"I'll need a couple of months."

"That long?"

"I'll need to locate the tools I need," Clint said. "That might entail some traveling. There's someone I know in New Mexico. And then I'll want to hand-deliver the gun."

"That, too, will entail traveling," Bollinger pointed out.

"Yes."

"Is that included in the two months?"

"It is."

Bollinger nodded.

"I'll let him know."

Clint stood up.

"Do we have a deal then, Mr. Bollinger?"

The attorney put his hand out.

"We have a deal."

Clint wished that the deal did not include shaking the man's hand again.

After dinner Clint and Hartman went back to Rick's Place, where they sat in the back at Hartman's private table.

Hartman had one of the girls bring over a bottle of champagne, at which time Clint also asked for a beer.

"I'm not paying for champagne," he said to Hartman.

"The champagne is on me, Clint," Hartman said, pouring two glasses. "You're gettin' a lot of money to do something you love, build a gun. That's worth a celebration."

"Thanks, Rick."

They each sipped and Clint put his glass down. He was not very partial to champagne and was waiting for the beer.

"You know," Hartman said, putting his glass down, "you probably could have got even more money."

"Maybe," Clint said, "but it's really not about the money, is it?"

"No, I guess not," Hartman said, "not for you, anyway. That's the biggest difference between you and me, though."

"What is?"

Hartman smiled.

"For me it's always about the money."

Clint smiled back and said, "Big surprise."

SIX

"When will you be leaving?" Priscilla asked, later that night.

"In the morning."

"So soon?"

"It's an important commission, Pris," Clint said. "I want to get started on it."

"I can understand that," she said. "It's just that . . ."

"What?"

She crawled into the circle of his arms and he held her tightly.

"I thought you'd be around longer this time."

"Priscilla," he said, "I've been here for weeks. I don't usually stay longer than that."

"I know," she said, "I was just hoping this time would be different."

"Pris," he said, "we've talked about this—"

"Oh, don't worry," she said, "I'm not wanting you to stay around forever. I mean—hell, I'd get tired of

25

you pretty quick, you know."

"I know."

She pressed her lips to his neck and said, "Not tonight, though."

"No," he said, "not tonight."

They kissed then, her tongue slipping sweetly into his mouth. He slid his hand between her legs and found her wet and ready, even though they had made love only twenty minutes ago.

He caressed her wetness with one finger, feeling her body tense. When he used a second finger she arched her back and drummed her heels on the bed.

"Ooh, God, you make me crazy when you do that. You have the *gentlest* touch . . ."

She rolled onto her back, and he leaned down to take her right nipple into his mouth. He rolled it around while continuing to touch her with his fingers.

"I want you inside me now or I'll *scream* . . ."

In Montana, Gloria Dain was thinking the same thing about Del Nolan, her husband's foreman. Nolan was a ripe thirty years old. His body was lean and hard, dun brown, where her husband's was pale and soft. Nolan had everything she liked in a man . . . except money. That Lawrence Dain had.

"Now, Del, now, damn it," she said.

Nolan straddled her and drove his rigid penis into her as if it were a battering ram. There were times when she had to slow him down, but this was not one of them. This time she wanted him to take her hard and fast, and hard . . . and harder . . .

"Harder, Del. Harder!"

Nolan had been her lover for the past three months. All that time she had been using sex to gain his loyalty. He had been working for her husband for several years but had only recently—four months ago—become the foreman of the ranch, promoted when the previous foreman, Ted Granger, died. Granger had been in his fifties, a contemporary of Lawrence Dain's. He had run the ranch for over fifteen years, freeing Dain to enjoy other things—like collecting guns.

Gloria had noticed Nolan when she first came to the ranch three years ago but had not approached him until he became foreman. She saw in him not only a lover—although she desperately needed one—but an ally.

"Yes, Del, yes, that's it," she said, as she felt her orgasm nearing.

Nolan, mindless in his pursuit of his own release, slid his hands beneath her to cup her buttocks so that he could drive into her even harder.

Nolan had not been a very skillful lover three months ago, and although he had learned a lot from Gloria Dain during that time, he still had a lot more to learn. Once she had her husband's money she wouldn't need him anymore. She'd use the money to travel and find more experienced lovers to see to her needs. For now, though, stuck on this ranch in Montana, Del Nolan was the best she could do. He was young, strong, eager, and ready to do whatever she wanted him to.

Now all she had to do was figure out what that was.

Priscilla was sitting astride Clint, and he watched in fascination as beads of sweat slid down between her breasts. He followed their progress over her belly—one lodged in her navel—and then beyond, where they were lost in the tangle his pubic hair made meshing with hers.

Priscilla was grunting with effort as she rode him hard, sliding up and then dropping down heavily on him, driving him deeply inside of her. If this was to be their last night together for a while, she was determined to make it one to remember.

Finally, when he couldn't take it anymore, he rolled them over so that he was on top and took control of the tempo. He worked her until she was whipping her head back and forth on the pillow and begging him to finish, and then he exploded inside of her. . . .

In the morning Clint slid from the bed quietly, without waking her. He knew that when she woke and found him gone she'd be angry at him for not waking her, but he'd be miles away by then, safe from her wrath. He also knew that if he did wake her he wouldn't be able to get out of the room for at least another hour and he wanted to get under way shortly after first light.

The evening before Clint had talked to the liveryman, instructing him to have his team, rig, and Duke ready by first light. He had paid the man extra to get up that early and see to it. When he arrived at the livery he saw that his money had been well spent.

"Here they are, all ready, like I promised," the liveryman said.

"Thanks, Jake. I appreciate it."

"Where you headin' this time?"

Duke was tied to the back of the rig. Clint climbed up into the seat.

"New Mexico, to see an old friend."

Jake, who was somewhere between sixty and eighty, said, "That's good. Old friends is the best."

"I agree, Jake."

"Course," Jake said to himself, as Clint rode away, "they's the only kind I got anymore."

SEVEN

Mick Bolton lived in Chula, New Mexico. He had a house a few miles outside of town, an adobe structure he had built himself to accommodate his chosen line of work. That had been over twenty years ago. Since then he had gotten married—an unexpected turn of events, to be sure—and he and his wife, Maria, proceeded to produce children at an alarming rate. Presently they had eight of their own, ranging from age nineteen to two months. They also had five others they had adopted, for one reason or another, ranging from abandonment to taking in runaways. These five were ages fifteen, twelve, nine, five, and three. Of the thirteen children who lived there, eight were girls, and five were boys. The oldest, the nineteen year old, was a beautiful girl named Candida.

Over the years Bolton had built extension after extension onto his house. The original structure was one huge room for him to work in and two smaller rooms in the back. The house now had twelve rooms spread out over two stories.

Clint had not been to Mick Bolton's home in over five years. That was six children—three born, three adopted—and four rooms ago.

As he rode up to the house he saw children running around, laughing and playing. Off to one side two women were hanging laundry. He didn't remember two women living there, and some quick math told him that Bolton's oldest son would only be about twelve or thirteen now. Certainly not old enough to have gotten married.

As he came closer the children noticed him and ran to the two women, who both turned. He recognized Bolton's wife. The young woman next to her looked to be about eighteen or nineteen. When they saw him they both smiled identical, beautiful smiles.

Clint reined in his team and stared at the two women and the half a dozen kids, half boys and half girls.

"My God," he said, suddenly recognizing the younger woman, "is that Candida?"

"Hello, Clint," the young woman said.

Clint dropped down from the rig and took Maria into his arms for a welcoming hug.

"Why did you not tell us you were coming?" she asked.

"I did," he said. "I sent Mick a telegram."

"But you did not say you were coming so soon. Mick will be thrilled."

Maria stepped aside so Clint could get a better look at Candida.

"She has grown up, no?" the proud mother asked.

"She has, indeed."

Candida laughed and rushed to hug Clint, who did not know quite what to do with this very grown-up Candida. The girl he remembered was thirteen or so. This woman was pressing full, firm breasts into his chest and he felt some confusion. Finally, he simply hugged her the way he had hugged her mother, then held her at arm's length.

"You're as beautiful as your mother," he said.

"That cannot be," Candida said. "Momma is the most beautiful woman in the world."

"You've been listening to your father."

"Come," Maria said again. "Mick will be so thrilled."

"Who are all these little ones?" Clint asked. He followed the two women, and the children followed behind them.

"We have added to the family since you were here last," Maria said.

"More babies?"

"We were blessed with three more births, and we adopted three more."

"My God," Clint said, "how many do you have now, altogether?"

"Thirteen," Maria said, "including the new *niño*."

"What new baby?"

"A boy," Maria said, "two months old."

Clint looked at Maria in surprise. Though still as beautiful as ever, perhaps more so, she had to be at least forty, not the ideal age for having a baby. And Mick was older than his wife by at least ten or twelve years. A fifty-year-old new father?

They led Clint into the house.

"You've added rooms, as well," he said, feeling as if he was going through a maze.

"Three," Maria said.

"Four, Momma," Candida said.

As they entered the main room where Bolton did all his work, the first room he had ever built, the smaller children pushed past and rushed into it, calling out, "Poppa, Poppa . . ."

Mick Bolton looked up from his work, first seeing the small children, then the two women, and finally—while he was hugging all six little ones at once—spotting Clint.

"Clint Adams!" he bellowed.

Mick Bolton was a big man who, for as long as Clint had known him, had a full beard that extended down over his chest. He stood up and rushed Clint, who steeled himself for a bone-crushing bear hug. Bolton was six foot six, tall enough to lift Clint clean off his feet while hugging him.

"You're breaking me, you big oaf!" Clint complained.

Bolton put Clint down and backed away.

"What do you think of the place now, huh?"

"More rooms, more kids . . ." Clint said.

"And more equipment," Bolton said proudly. "You'll be able to build a beautiful weapon here, Clint." He turned to his wife before Clint had a chance to respond and said, "Prepare a feast, Maria, and a room. Our friend will be here for a while."

EIGHT

Over dinner Mick and Maria Bolton reintroduced Clint to the children he hadn't seen in five years, and then introduced him to the new children. By the time the meal had ended all of the children were chattering at him as if they had known him for years—all but one. He noticed uncomfortably that Candida was sitting at the far end of the table, staring at him. Under any other circumstances he would have welcomed the attentions of a young lady so beautiful, but this was his friend's daughter. Clint usually stayed away from friends' wives and daughters.

After dinner Maria and Candida cleared the table and the other children were shooed away so that Bolton and Clint could have coffee and talk.

"I've got everything you need," Bolton told him, "and if you need my help, I'm here."

"I think this is something I'm going to want to do myself, Mick."

"I understand, Clint," Bolton said. "I just want you to know that you can use everything I have here, even me."

"I appreciate it, Mick."

"How long do you figure this will take?"

"I have no idea."

"Well, what kind of gun were you figuring on building?"

"I have no idea."

"How much thought have you put into this?"

"A lot."

"I can tell."

"Look," Clint said, "all I know for sure is that Dain wants a pistol."

"Well, that's a good start."

"His whole collection is made up of pistols," Clint said. "He's got one that was made for him by Sam Colt."

"That's impressive."

"I know."

"But what kind of gun is it?"

"What?"

"Do you know what kind of gun it is?"

Clint hesitated, then said, "A pistol, I guess."

"You see?"

Clint stared at Bolton.

"Do I see what?" he asked, confused.

"It's not what kind of gun it is," Bolton said, "it's who made it. Do you understand?"

Clint smiled.

"Yes, Mick," he said, "I understand."

"Good," Bolton said, "now let's go and look at my workshop. I'll show you around."

By the time Clint reached Chula, New Mexico, Henry Bollinger had returned to Montana and was talking to Lawrence Dain in his office. Neither of them knew that Gloria Dain was standing outside in the hallway, listening to their conversation.

"What was the final agreed upon price?" Dain asked Bollinger.

The attorney gave him the amount. Out in the hall Gloria Dain flinched, but behind the desk Lawrence Dain did not.

"I would have paid more."

"I know that," Bollinger said, "and so did he."

"Then why did he agree?"

Bollinger shrugged.

"He must have had his own reasons."

"Maybe you were reading him wrong, Henry," Dain said. "Maybe he just wasn't smart enough to know he could have gotten more."

"I doubt that," Bollinger said. "My take on him is that he's a very intelligent man."

Dain couldn't accept that. If Adams knew that he could have gotten more money and he didn't push for it, that was something he couldn't understand. It could only mean a lack of intelligence on the man's part. That really didn't matter, though. The only thing that mattered was that he was getting a gun built by Clint Adams, and he was getting it at a good price.

•   •   •

Outside in the hall Gloria Dain was feeling dizzy. She couldn't believe that her husband was going to pay that much for a gun—*another* gun. And he didn't even balk at the price. Good God, he had expected to pay more!

When she heard the meeting breaking up she hurried down the hall and into the den. Even as she ran, though, her legs felt weak, not from fear but from anger. How could he just give that much money away for . . . for a toy! That's what guns were for men, toys.

Her first thought was to confront Dain, but she knew what would happen. He would shoo her away and tell her that his business was not her business— only she didn't consider this to be business.

This was a waste.

She decided not to talk to her husband about it. She had another man to talk to.

"All right, Henry," Dain said, "you can go."

"I think you should understand, Lawrence, that Clint Adams is an intelligent man—"

"Intelligent men don't walk away from money, Henry," Dain said.

"But I think—"

"That's enough, Henry," Dain said, more firmly. "I have things to do, and so do you."

Bollinger stared at his employer for a few moments and then stood up. Obviously Dain wasn't going to listen to reason, so there was no use talking to him. What was the difference, anyway?

Then he remembered . . .

"Oh, one more thing, Lawrence."

"What's that?"

"Mr. Adams wants to hand-deliver the weapon when it's finished."

"Excellent," Dain said. "I'll look forward to meeting him."

Bollinger left the office, wondering how Clint Adams would react to being treated like something less than the smart man that he was.

It would be an interesting meeting to observe.

Gloria decided to intercept Bollinger at the front door, as she had the last time he was there.

"Hello, Gloria," Bollinger said. As always, when confronted with her beauty, he began to sweat, and she noticed.

"I understand Mr. Adams has agreed to build the weapon for Lawrence."

"That's right," Bollinger said cautiously. He didn't know how Gloria knew about this, or how much she knew.

"And Mr. Adams will be coming here when he's finished the gun?"

"That's right."

"Well, that should be interesting," she said. "When will he be coming?"

"I'm not sure, Gloria," Bollinger said, "but he seems to think he'll need a couple of months to build the gun and then travel here."

"From Texas?"

"No," Bollinger said, before he could stop himself, "from New Mexico."

"Ah," Gloria said. She almost asked him where in

New Mexico, but she could see by the look on his face that he thought he'd already given away too much. "We'll have to have a dinner party for him when he arrives."

"That would be . . . nice," the lawyer said.

"And you'll have to come, Henry," she added. "Make a note of it for yourself, will you?"

"Of course, Gloria."

"Well," she said, "I'm keeping you. It was nice seeing you."

"And you," he said, "as always."

As he went out the door she was already trying to figure out how to find out exactly where in New Mexico Clint Adams was.

NINE

Clint was in Mick Bolton's workshop, just getting himself acquainted with the way it was set up when Candida walked in carrying a cup.

"I brought you some coffee."

"Thank you, Candida. That's real nice of you."

She handed it to him and made no move to leave.

"Black and strong, just the way you like it."

"You remember that?"

"I was fourteen when you were last here, Clint," she said. "I wasn't a little girl. I remember a lot of things about you."

"You do, do you?"

It was afternoon, the day after he had arrived. The children had all been given breakfast separate from him and Bolton, and that included Candida. This was the first time he had seen her since dinner last night. For some reason the fact that she was a beautiful young woman now was very disconcerting to him.

Also, it seemed apparent to him that she liked him, and not just as her father's friend. Had she had a crush on him when she was fourteen? He truthfully didn't remember. Now, however, she was a full grown woman of nineteen, and a crush would be something he'd have to deal with. He didn't feel he could talk to Bolton about it, so maybe he should have a talk with Maria.

"Yes, I do."

"Hmmm," he said, not wanting to ask what she remembered. He sipped the coffee and said, "This is good. Did you make it?"

"Yes, I did, and I can cook, too."

"That's, um, good."

He didn't like where the conversation was going, so he was very glad when Maria came into the room.

"Candida?" she called. "There is work to be done."

Clint saw Candida make a face just before she turned to her mother.

"I just brought Clint a cup of coffee, Momma."

"Well, now that you have brought it you can get back to work."

"Yes, Momma." She turned to Clint and said, "I will see you at dinner."

"See you then."

She hurried past her mother and out of the room. Maria approached Clint, studying him.

"She makes me nervous," he admitted.

She laughed.

"You, who have had so many women? Made nervous by a slip of a girl?"

"She's not a slip of a girl, Maria," Clint said. "She's a grown woman."

"To you," Maria said, "to me and to her father she is still a girl."

"I am keeping that in mind, Maria."

"She likes you, Clint."

"Well—"

"She liked you when she was fourteen. In fact . . . I should not be telling you this . . . . when she was fourteen she told me that she was going to marry you."

"Fourteen-year-old girls," Clint said, shaking his head, trying to brush the remark off.

"Not only when she was fourteen," Maria went on. "She has mentioned it at least once every year, whenever your name came up."

"Really."

"Yes."

"Has she, uh, mentioned it to Mick?"

"No," Maria said, "only to me."

"Well, that's good."

"She might mention it to him while you are here, though."

"Why do you say that?" he asked.

"Because," Maria said, "she told it to me again last night."

TEN

Gloria contrived to meet with the foreman, Del Nolan, later that same day. Since Nolan had his own quarters, she was often able to slip into them unnoticed. They had sex and she was particularly avid so as to wear him out. She wanted him in a weakened condition when she talked to him about stealing, and maybe even killing.

Toward the end she slid down between his legs, took his penis in her hands, and began to lick and suck it. She brought him to the brink of orgasm several times, only to stop, and when she finally coaxed him over the edge he groaned aloud and lifted his buttocks off the bed, so forceful was his ejaculation.

She snuggled up to him then, pressed her head to his chest so that she could feel how rapidly his heart was beating.

"If you and your husband were still having sex," he said, "that would have killed him."

One of the things she lied to him about was her sex life with her husband. The truth was that she had sex with Dain about three times a week, and although it was always very unsatisfying to her, she knew that Dain enjoyed it just fine. All men did. They thought all they had to do was poke it into a woman a few times, grunt and roll over, and everyone was happy.

"That's why I'm glad I have you around," she said, and then added for effect, "my big, strong man."

He held her tightly then, believing every word she said. Why was it, she wondered, that younger men were more gullible than the older ones? She didn't even think that Dain was foolish enough to think that she married him because she really loved him. He wanted a pretty wife, and she wanted what she thought would be an easy life, married to a wealthy man. Well, he got what he wanted, but she sure didn't get what she was looking for.

She was still trying.

"Del?"

"Hmm?"

"Remember all that talking we've done—"

"What talking?" he asked, without letting her finish. He did that a lot, spoke before she was done. She had to fight to keep her patience sometimes.

"You know. About my husband dying and us living in the house together."

"Oh, that," he said. "That's just silly talk."

"Not so silly," she said. "It could happen."

"Is he feeling sick?"

What a dope, she thought.

"No, he's not feeling sick."

"Well then, how would that happen? If he's healthy he could live for a long time. He's not *that* old, you know."

"I know," she said. "He's old enough to last a long time, long enough for him to spend all his money."

"Is he spending more money?"

"Yes."

"On what?"

"On what else?" she asked. "A gun."

"Another one?"

"Yes."

"What's so special about this one?"

"It's being built for him by Clint Adams."

"The Gunsmith?"

"That's right."

Nolan whistled softly in the dark.

"He must be paying a lot for that."

"Too much," she said. "Del?"

"What?"

"I'd give anything if he didn't get that gun."

Nolan laughed.

"And how do you think that could happen?"

"Well," she said, "if somebody knew when Adams was coming with the gun, and where he was coming from, they could take it from him."

"Take a gun from the Gunsmith? That's a lot easier said than done, Gloria."

"Not so hard," she said. "After all, he's not as young as he used to be."

"A man would have to be a fool to try something like that," Nolan said.

She had her fool, all she had to do was convince him. To that end she slid her hand down between his legs and took hold of him . . .

ELEVEN

Mick Bolton found Clint sitting on one of the house's three sets of stairs.

"What are you doin' here?" Bolton asked.

"Thinking."

"Dinner is almost ready." Bolton sat a few steps above Clint. "What are you thinkin' about, my friend?"

"This gun I'm supposed to build," Clint said. "I've been here a week and I haven't even started yet."

"Well, once you decide what you're going to do it shouldn't take that long, not with the equipment at your disposal."

"I suppose."

"What's wrong, Clint?"

"What do you mean?"

"Everythin' is ready for you," Bolton said. "I've got barrels of all shapes and sizes, hammers, files, drills, all the tools you'd need."

Clint did not reply.

"Everythin' is ready but you. Why?"

Clint turned and looked up at his friend.

"I don't know that I'm up to the task, Mick."

"What are you talkin' about?" Bolton asked. "You're one of the finest gunsmiths I've ever known."

"I haven't made a weapon in a long time," Clint said. "You're *the* finest gunsmith I've ever known. Maybe you should do it."

"I'd be happy to, Clint, and then you can deliver it—" Bolton started.

"No, no," Clint said, "you don't understand. Jesus, I'd never take credit for your work, Mick. No, I mean you should make this damned gun. I can send Dain a telegraph message telling him that you'll do it—"

"You can't do that."

"Why not?"

"Because he wants a gun made by you, not by me," Bolton said.

"A gun made by you would be the best weapon in his collection."

"A gun made by me would mean nothing to him," Bolton said. "He wants a weapon made by the Gunsmith. That's what he's payin' for."

"That's another thing."

"What?"

"Does he really care how well the gun is made?" Clint asked. "Or does he just want to display a gun made by me?"

"Why does that matter?" Bolton asked. "If you're gonna make the gun, you're gonna do the best job you can. It don't matter what he wants, or thinks."

Bolton reached out and put one of his huge hands on Clint's shoulder.

"My friend, take my word for it, all you've got to do is get started."

"I suppose so."

"Unfortunately," Bolton said, looking at the sky, "the light's gonna be gone in a while, and good lighting is the most important thing. You're not gonna be able to start until tomorrow."

"Okay."   ·

"But tomorrow for sure, right?" Bolton squeezed Clint's shoulder as he asked.

"Ow, yeah, tomorrow," Clint said, "if you don't break my shoulder first."

Bolton let up the pressure but slapped Clint on the back for good measure.

"Come on, dinner's ready."

"All right," Clint said, standing and arching his back.

"Candida's anxious to show off her cooking skills," Bolton said.

"Uh, Candida cooked tonight?"

"She did," Bolton said proudly. "My little girl's quite a cook, Clint."

"I'm sure she is, Mick."

"Some man is gonna be real lucky to have her as a wife."

"Uh-huh."

"Course, that won't be for a while."

"Right," Clint agreed, following Bolton through the house, "not for a long while."

TWELVE

As it turned out Candida was indeed a fabulous cook. She had prepared several different dishes: tortillas, fajitas, a huge pot of red rice, and at least four different vegetables, not to mention biscuits.

Clint did the meal justice, stuffing himself while Bolton beamed proudly. They sat at a big, long wooden table that Bolton had built especially for his family, so that the sixteen of them could all eat at the same time. The table was in a covered area of the house that had no walls, so essentially they were eating outdoors.

After dinner and before coffee Bolton produced a bottle of tequila and brandished it at Clint.

"This is for you and me to finish tonight, my friend," he said.

"The whole bottle?"

"What's the matter?" Bolton asked. "Afraid that I'll drink you under the table?"

"That'll be the day, you big galoot."

Bolton unstopped the bottle and said, "Well, let's see, then."

Halfway through the tequila they decided that it would be nice if they had some beer, too.

"Surprise, surprise," Bolton said.

"What?"

Bolton stood up and staggered away. When he came back he was carrying a keg of beer on his shoulder as if it were weightless.

"I've been keeping this for a special occasion."

"But we'll have it now, anyway, right?" Clint said.

"Right," Bolton said, putting the keg down next to the table. Clint tested its weight with his foot and knew he never would have been able to lift it himself.

"I'll get some mugs," Bolton said.

He returned and poured two mugs full of beer, handed one to Clint.

"It's warm," Bolton said, "but it'll still do its job."

They finished the tequila and drank half the keg of beer and neither was willing to give in.

Maria came into the room and studied them both, her hands on her hips.

"Are you two not yet drunk enough to go to bed?" she asked.

They stared at each other, squinting to see across the table.

"Don't know," Bolton said.

"We haven't tried to get up yet," Clint said.

"Well, from the look of your eyes I don't think you should."

Bolton looked at Clint.

"She doesn't think we can get up."

Clint looked at Bolton and said, "You know what? I agree with her."

"Ah," Bolton said, making a face, "I can get up with no problem."

"Be my guest," Clint said.

Bolton put both of his massive hands down flat on the table and pushed up. As he stood, Clint could see that he wasn't going to make it. It was in his eyes, and in his balance.

"Mick, don't—" he said, but it was too late. His friend was toppling over. Maria shouted and Clint tried to get up to catch him, but his own legs weren't working so well.

Bolton hit the floor and shook the place for a moment. Clint leaned over in his chair and stared at his friend, who was breathing normally.

"Is he all right?" Maria asked.

"He's fine," Clint said, "but I think he's going to spend the night there."

"What about you?" she asked.

Clint frowned and got slowly to his feet. He stood there for a moment, and when he didn't fall over he smiled, looked at Maria, and said, "I guess I won."

Maria shook her head and left the room, muttering, "Little boy games."

THIRTEEN

Clint woke in the morning and didn't think he'd be able to get out of bed. Before he knew it, though, he was standing, and didn't remember doing it. Dimly, the events of the previous night came back to him. He had left Mick Bolton where he lay, practically under the table, and had staggered to his room and bed. Now he felt he had to go and see if he could wake Bolton and get him into his own bed.

He left his room and made his way to the dining area where he was shocked to find Bolton not only sitting up but having breakfast. The smell of the food forced a wave of nausea through his stomach.

"Coffee?" Maria asked, as she poured her husband another cup. Bolton looked as if he was wearing the same clothes as the night before.

"I—I've got to take a bath," Clint said, his voice raspy.

Maria smiled.

"I'll have coffee ready when you get out of the bath," she said. "Do you want anything else?"

"Come on, Clint," Bolton said, "have some eggs."

Clint rushed from the room before his stomach betrayed him.

Later he returned to find Bolton still eating.

"Coffee?" Maria asked again.

Clint was feeling slightly more human so he said, "Yes, please."

"No eggs?" Bolton asked.

Clint waved the suggestion away.

"No eggs." He accepted the cup of coffee from Maria. "How can you eat after last night?"

"Easy," Bolton said. "I'm hungry." The big man pointed with his fork. "Maybe you drank me under the table, but I can still eat you under the table, anytime."

"I believe you," Clint said. "You must have a cast-iron stomach."

"You eat very well," Maria said, patting her husband's broad shoulders, "but you smell like a goat. Go and take a bath."

"I'm not finished eatin'," Bolton complained.

"You are finished," his wife told him. "Go."

"See how she treats me?" Bolton asked Clint as he stood up. "Be grateful you never got married."

"And I won't ever get married," Clint said, "because you got the last good one."

Bolton waved a hand and left the room.

Maria sat opposite Clint and put her hand over his.

"You are good for him," she said.

"How? By getting him drunk?"

"He has not gotten drunk in a long time," she said. "Years."

"Why not?"

"It is difficult for a man to relax when he has such a family to support."

"He loves all of you, Maria."

"Oh, I know that," she said, waving his words away. "I have no doubt that Mick loves me and all the children, but he still needs to relax every once in a while. He can only do that with a good friend."

"Doesn't Mick have any friends?"

She smiled.

"Lots of friends," she said, "but none so good as you."

"Oh yeah," Clint said, "I'm such a good friend that I haven't been around for five or six years."

"We all have different lives," she said wisely.

"And we come into each other's lives only when we need something?"

"You are too hard on yourself," she said, patting his hand. "You needed help and Mick was here to give it to you. When we need help, you will be there."

"I will?"

"Of that I have no doubt," she said. She saw that his cup was empty. "I will get you some more coffee, and then I have my work, and you have yours."

Yes, he thought, he did have his work to do, and it was about time he did it.

FOURTEEN

Vic Lennon wanted Gloria Dain.

He had wanted Gloria Dain from the first moment Lawrence Dain brought her home as his new wife. He had only been working at the Dain ranch a few months when this happened, after three long years of traveling and making his way as well as he could. Once he saw Gloria, though, he knew he'd be staying at the Dain ranch for a while, and that was what he did. He stayed. He waited. He bided his time.

Until now.

Lennon knew what was going on between Del Nolan and Gloria, and he knew that Nolan was not man enough for her. He wouldn't be able to keep her satisfied any more than her husband could. Soon, very soon, she'd be turning her eyes elsewhere, and that's when Lennon would make his move.

In fact, Lennon had started even before that. He had befriended Del Nolan just about the same time Gloria had. That way he was able to keep tabs on their relationship.

For the past few months Nolan had been talking to Lennon about his affair with the boss's wife. Even though Nolan was the foreman, Lennon was the older man, and Nolan often asked him for advice.

"She's startin' to talk crazy, Vic," Nolan said.

"Like how?"

"Like talkin' about the boss dyin' and all."

"Well, that could happen."

"Yeah, but I think . . ."

"You think what?"

Nolan looked around, even though no one else was near enough to hear them. They were standing by the stable, just the two of them, while the other men were performing their chores.

"I think she's gonna ask me to kill him."

Lennon found this very interesting.

"What makes you think that?"

"Well . . . I shouldn't even be tellin' you this."

"Come on, Del. We're friends, ain't we?"

"Yeah . . . I guess it's okay."

What a dope, Lennon thought, without knowing that this was exactly the same thought Gloria Dain had had so many times.

"She's already asked me to rob Clint Adams."

"Clint Adams, the Gunsmith?"

Nolan nodded.

"Why does she want to rob him?"

Nolan told Lennon the story of Lawrence Dain paying Clint Adams a lot of money to build a gun for him.

"And she wants you to rob Adams?"

"Right."

"Of what?"

"Of the gun."

"What about the money?"

"She didn't mention the money."

"Well, it would be a shame to rob him of the gun and not the money, Del."

"I don't want to rob him of anything," Nolan said.

"Look, kid, you want to keep the woman, don't ya?" Lennon asked.

"Well—"

"Sure you do," Lennon said, "and the only way to do that is to do what she wants."

"But, Vic—"

"Hell, I'd even help ya."

"You would?"

"Sure." Lennon clapped Nolan on the back and asked, "What are friends for?"

"But . . . Jesus, we're talkin' about Clint Adams here, Vic."

"So what? He's only one man, ain't he?"

"Well, yeah . . ."

"And there'd be two of us, maybe more."

"More?"

"Sure," Lennon said. "I know of two good boys who'd go along with us. That would make it four against one. Even the Gunsmith can't buck those kinds of odds, can he?"

"Well . . ."

"Sure he can't," Lennon said. "Listen, the next time you talk to Mrs. Gloria Dain this is what you tell her . . ."

"You'll do it?" Gloria asked Del Nolan.

"Yeah."

In the darkness of his room she couldn't see the look of indecision on his face.

"Really?"

"If you want me to."

"Oh, Del," she said, pressing her naked body more tightly against his, "it's just to teach Lawrence a lesson. He shouldn't be spending all that money on a gun."

"I know."

"That's our money, Del."

"I know."

"Oh, darling, you've made me so happy."

She slid atop him and showed him how happy she was.

Later, in her own room, Gloria Dain stood at the window looking outside. She knew that Del Nolan had been talked into her plan by someone else. He did, after all, say that he'd have help. Gloria figured that Nolan had been talking to someone, someone who saw that her idea was a sound one. One of the other men on the ranch was controlling Nolan from one side while she was controlling him from the other. If she could find that man they could work together on this.

But who could it be?

FIFTEEN

Clint decided to make the pistol double-action rather than single. It didn't really make a difference, since Lawrence Dain was probably never going to fire the weapon, but Clint decided to build it as if he was going to use it himself. In fact, it was going to be based on his own Colt, which he had long ago modified from single-action to double-action. He guessed that made it a double modification of a Colt.

He had been working on the gun for a week now and already he realized that he was going to be finished way ahead of schedule. He'd decided, though, that even if he was finished ahead of schedule he wasn't going to deliver it that far in advance. He didn't want Lawrence Dain thinking he had paid too much and wasn't getting his money's worth on labor.

To Mick Bolton's credit he had stayed out of Clint's way when Clint was using the workshop. Luckily—for Clint, anyway—the man did not presently have any commissions of his own, so Clint was able to take his time.

In the evenings, though, Clint spent time with Bolton and Maria and their family. He played with the little kids, told stories to the older ones, and fenced verbally with Candida. Often she would stop and sit next to him to talk to him, and he would pretend not to know what she was getting at. He was also nervous about Bolton finding out about them—even though there was nothing to find out. Candida obviously found him attractive, and he certainly found her attractive, but he intended to do nothing at all about it.

He didn't know what Candida's intentions were, though, beyond the fact that she'd told her mother she was going to marry him. Clint wondered if the young woman intended to wait until he proposed, or if she was going to propose, herself.

He also noticed the amused looks on Maria Bolton's face when she saw Clint and Candida together. She was enjoying his discomfort. He wondered if Maria had said anything to Mick Bolton. The big man hadn't said anything to him, nor did he seem particularly interested whenever Clint and Candida were talking.

Clint was finishing up his day's work when Mick Bolton came into the room.

"Hi, Mick," he said. "I was just finishing up. I think it might be ready to test fire tomorrow."

Bolton came over and looked at the weapon, which was sitting in a vise.

"It's beautiful."

The gun was blue/black metal with pale ivory sidings on the butt.

"I see you decided not to go with his initials," Bolton observed.

"Okay, okay," Clint said sheepishly, "so I went a little overboard with that idea, but what do you think of this?"

"I think it's beautiful work . . . but will it shoot straight?"

"Not that Lawrence Dain will ever find out, but we'll find out, maybe tomorrow, huh?"

"Maybe we can have a little fun, eh?"

"What kind of fun?"

"Oh, I don't know," Bolton said, "maybe put on a little show for the family."

"Can you still shoot?" Clint asked. "I thought old age had robbed you of your steady hand and eye."

"You'll see how much old age has robbed me of," Bolton said. "You use your new gun, there, and let me use your old one."

Clint's "old" gun was sitting in his holster, which was in his room. He was so comfortable around his old friend's house that he had taken to not wearing the gun at all.

"Today's Tuesday," Clint said. "Give me until Thursday and you've got yourself a date."

"Thursday it is," Bolton said. "I hope that gun shoots as good as it looks."

"It'll shoot as good as the man holding it," Clint promised.

Bolton smiled broadly and said, "We'll just see about that, won't we?"

SIXTEEN

Vic Lennon.

It had to be.

Gloria Dain was sitting on the porch where all the men could see her. She enjoyed doing this because she knew that most of the men couldn't help but watch her. Sometimes she fantasized that the men would go by and she would eventually pick one of them, take him inside to her bed and make love with him. There were several of the men she wouldn't have minded bedding. Of course, most of them had worked for her husband for a long time, but she liked the idea of testing their loyalty by appearing naked in front of them.

Del Nolan's loyalty had certainly wilted in the face of her pale, naked flesh.

For the past ten days she had been watching the men, trying to figure out who besides her was pulling

Nolan's strings, and today she had come up with the answer.

Vic Lennon.

She had two reasons for picking Lennon. One, he never looked at her. Not ever. It was for that very reason that she knew he wanted her.

And two, she noticed that the two of them spent a lot of time together talking.

Lennon was about eight years older than Nolan, but in terms of actual experience he probably had twenty years on the young foreman. He was tall and lanky, usually dressed in dark clothes, and always wore a gun, even around the ranch. He was obviously a man of action, and Gloria couldn't figure out what he'd been doing working on the ranch for the past three years or more.

In the three years that she had been there she didn't think any words had ever passed between them. She also didn't know why she hadn't really noticed him before. She noticed him now, though. She liked the way he moved, and the way he ignored her. She found him interesting, and she was sure that he was the kind of man who would do what she wanted for the same reasons. She wouldn't have to try to fool him into stealing, or even killing.

Vic Lennon.

It was time for her to get to know Lennon a lot better.

Lennon had been expecting it.

He had seen how Gloria was showing herself

more often on the porch. He knew she did that sometimes just to tease the men. They all slobbered over her, said how lucky the boss was to have such a beautiful wife. They all wondered how she'd be in bed, while none of them would ever have the nerve to find out.

Del Nolan knew how she was, but it hadn't taken nerve. She had targeted him and reeled him in, and it was his own foolishness that got him involved with a woman he just couldn't handle.

Lennon, on the other hand, made a point of ignoring her. He knew that one day soon she'd be his, so let the others step on their tongues and give her the attention she wanted.

That's the way it had been for the past three years, but lately he'd noticed something. *She* was paying more attention to *him*. Why was that? Could it be because they had Del Nolan in common?

He now felt sure that Gloria was going to make a move. She was going to make a point of talking to him. She was a smart woman. Maybe she knew, instinctively, that it wasn't she who had talked Nolan into going along with her idea but someone else. And once she figured that out, how long would it take her to figure out who the other party was?

Not long, not long at all.

Three years of waiting was about to come to an end, and none too soon. He was almost tired of waiting for her. He was certainly tired of working as a cowhand. There were two ways to change that. One was to leave and hit the trail again.

The other was to get his hands on some Dain money.

SEVENTEEN

"Clint?"

"Yes, Candida?"

"Do you like me?"

It was after dinner and she had finished helping her mother clean the kitchen. After coffee with Bolton, Clint had stepped outside to get some night air and look at the moon. He was surprised when Candida came out to join him—surprised and nervous. He still couldn't get over the fact that a nineteen-year-old girl could make him so nervous. Of course, there was also the presence of her fifty-year-old—and six foot six—father to consider.

"Of course I like you," he said carefully. "I like your whole family."

"No," she said, "I mean, do you like me?"

He looked at her.

"I don't understand," he lied.

"You know what I mean," she said. "Do you like me . . . as a woman?"

Now he realized he was going to have to deal with this issue head-on. He only hoped that he could deal with it correctly.

"Candida, you're a very lovely girl—"

"Woman," she said, correcting him. "I am a woman now, Clint."

"Candida, you're nineteen, and you're my friend's daughter."

"And if I was not your friend's daughter?"

"Well, you'd still be only nineteen. I am a lot older than you."

"Poppa is older than Momma."

"I know, but the difference between their ages is not as great as the difference between ours."

"Why is age so important?" she asked.

"It just is."

"You don't love me?"

"Candida—"

"You don't want me?"

He turned to her.

"I want you as my friend," Clint said. "I've known you since you were a little girl. I can't think of you as a grown woman, Candida. I'm sorry."

She stared at him for a few moments, then her eyes began to fill and her chin started to tremble.

"Candida—" he started, but she turned and ran back into the house—right past her father.

"Is she cryin'?" he asked Clint.

"Uh—"

"She didn't go and tell you that fool thought she

has about marryin' you, did she?"

"You know about that?" Clint asked, surprised.

Bolton gave Clint a look and said, "I've known about that for years, since she was twelve or thirteen."

"She's not twelve or thirteen anymore, Mick," Clint said. "I didn't want to hurt her feelings."

"What's the matter?" Bolton asked. "My daughter ain't good enough for you to marry?"

Clint studied his friend for a moment to see if he was kidding. He honestly couldn't tell.

"She's a little too young for me, Mick."

"So?"

"She needs a man her own age."

"A boy, you mean," Bolton said, "a boy her own age. No, I think she needs somebody older."

"Not as old as me."

"Don't you think she's pretty?"

"She's beautiful, Mick, you know that," Clint said. "Look, I've known her too long. She'll always be a child to me."

Bolton took a moment to light his pipe.

"Did you tell her that?" he asked when he had it going to his satisfaction.

"Not in so many words, but yeah, I told her."

Bolton slapped Clint on the back and said, "Well then, don't worry about it. She'll get over it."

"I hope so," Clint said. "I don't want her to hate me."

"Nah, she'd never do that. You all ready to shoot tomorrow?"

"I'm ready."

"You gonna let me use your gun?"

"Sure."

"Then get ready to go down in defeat," Bolton said.

"What's the difference?" Clint asked. "We're just testing the gun."

"No, no, no," Bolton said, "if we're gonna shoot we got to be shootin' for somethin'."

"Like what?"

"Lemme think."

Bolton puffed on his pipe while he gave it some thought.

"Okay, I got it."

"What?"

"If you win I'll make you a brand-new rifle. One like you never seen before."

"Okay," Clint said. "And if I lose?"

"You marry my daughter."

"What?"

Once again he couldn't tell if the man was kidding.

"Hey, Clint, Maria and me would love to have you in the family."

"That's crazy," Clint said. "I'm not going to shoot for your daughter. I've got more respect for her than that."

"Afraid you're gonna lose?"

"Losing has nothing to do with it."

"Then it's a bet?"

"No," Clint said, "it's not a bet. Think of something else."

Clint got up from the step he was sitting on and said, "I'm going to bed. In the morning you can let me know what else you come up with."

"You're afraid of gettin' married, that's what it is," Bolton said.

"Aren't you the one who told me I was lucky I wasn't?" Clint asked.

"Oh, that," Bolton said, waving his hand, "I was just kiddin' about that. Marriage is great, and so is havin' kids."

"Not as many kids as you have."

"Hey," Bolton said, "how about if you lose you take some of my kids?"

"I'm going to bed," Clint said sternly. "Good night."

"Chicken," Bolton said to Clint's retreating back.

Clint waved his hand behind him in a gesture of dismissal and went into the house to his room. Kids were okay as long as they were somebody else's. He wasn't going to shoot against Bolton for his kids, or for his daughter's hand in marriage.

Jesus, if kids were so great why was Bolton trying to get rid of them?

EIGHTEEN

The next morning Clint woke feeling he had overstayed his welcome with Mick Bolton and his family. After all, Bolton was trying to marry him off to his daughter, or give him some of his kids. The gun was finally finished. If he left today or tomorrow, he could get to Montana a couple of weeks ahead of schedule. All the gun had to do was perform well that afternoon and he could be on his way.

He got dressed and strapped on his gun. Mick Bolton was one of the few men who Clint had ever let touch his gun. He'd worked on it on several occasions and had fired it once or twice to test it. Today would be the first time the man fired it in earnest.

He left his room and went down for breakfast. The family was already there, and all of the children greeted him warmly, as did Maria and Bolton. The only one who was cold to him was Candida, and he hoped it would not last long.

"Are you ready for today?" Bolton asked.

"Ready as I'll ever be," Clint said.

"When do you want to do this?"

"After breakfast is okay."

Bolton stared at Clint across the table.

"If it fires well you'll be leaving, won't you?"

"Yes."

"Today?"

"Yes."

"We'll be sorry to see you go, Clint," Maria said.

The smaller children echoed her sentiment. Candida simply looked away.

"It's time for me to get going," Clint said. "I can't stay in one place for very long."

"The woman who finally ties you down is gonna be some hellcat," Bolton said. He was oblivious to the looks the remark drew from both his daughter and his wife.

"I'm too old a dog to be tied down, Mick," Clint said.

"You're never getting married?" Maria asked.

"I don't think so, Maria."

"What a shame," she said. "You would make some woman a very fine husband."

Candida slammed down a pot and stormed out of the room.

"Give her time, Clint," Maria said. "She will get over it."

"Get over what?" one of the other children asked.

"Never mind," Maria said. "Eat your breakfast."

•   •   •

After breakfast Clint went into the workshop to get the gun. It was still in the vise where he had left it. He loosened the vise, removed the gun, and walked outside. Bolton and some of his sons were setting up targets made up of bottles of varying sizes. As Clint approached, Bolton turned and extended his hand, palm up.

"Your gun, please."

Clint removed his gun from his holster and handed it to the man, then put the new gun in its place. He worked the gun in and out of the holster a few times, then took it out and tested the balance.

"How does it feel?" Bolton asked.

"It feels good," Clint said.

"Do you mind?"

Clint held the gun out to Bolton, who tucked the other gun into his belt before accepting it.

"It does feel good," he said, hefting it. "This is real fine work, Clint."

"Thanks."

Bolton handed it back.

"Now it's time to see if it can shoot straight."

Clint took some bullets from his gun belt and loaded the gun.

"You need a new gun," Bolton said, hefting Clint's gun.

"What's wrong with that one?" Clint said.

"Nothin'," Bolton said, "you could just use a new one."

"Well," Clint said, "all I have to do is outshoot you, and you can make me one. By the way, what do you get if I lose?"

Bolton looked at Clint, then down at the gun in his hand.

"How about this gun?" he asked. "If I outshoot you, I get this gun."

"You're confident," Clint said.

"No, I'm not," Bolton said. "I've just got nothin' to lose."

Clint thought it over.

"What do you say?"

Clint smiled.

"You're on."

NINETEEN

The whole family turned out for the contest. Even Candida came out to watch, standing off from the others with her arms folded beneath her breasts.

"Who shoots first?" Bolton asked.

"After you."

Bolton and his sons had set the bottles up at various distances. They shot at the nearest ones first. The distances were not great, because they were firing pistols, not rifles.

Bolton shattered his bottle with one shot and his children cheered. Clint shattered his and there was a smattering of applause.

Bolton stepped up and fired at his next bottle, smashing it cleanly. More shouts and applause. Clint fired, enjoying the feel of the new gun and relishing that the gun was firing straight and true.

They each shattered five bottles with no problem, leaving six to shoot at.

"We'd better reload," Bolton said.

"Take your last shot," Clint said, peering down at the targets.

Bolton sighted and fired and hit just enough of the bottle to break it.

"I'll reload while you shoot," Bolton said.

"Don't bother," Clint said.

"Whataya mean?"

"Look at the way you set up these bottles."

"What about it?" Bolton asked.

"Watch."

Clint walked to his left, keeping his eyes on the three remaining bottles. He stopped when he was sure that he was seeing them in a straight line. He knew Bolton hadn't done it on purpose, but from this angle all three bottles were lined up.

"What are you up to?" Bolton asked.

"Watch," Clint said.

He fired his last bullet. It shattered the first bottle, kept going and hit the second, and continued on to go through the third.

He broke all three bottles with one shot.

Clint turned and saw Bolton gaping at him. The family were all looking on in awe, as well.

"I don't believe that," Bolton said.

Clint ejected the shells from the new gun but did not bother to reload.

"They just happened to be set up the right way," Clint said.

Bolton was still staring.

"I don't think I could do that if I tried."

"Go ahead," Clint said. "You've got two bottles left."

Bolton frowned.

"If you can drill the last two bottles with one shot," Clint said, "we'll call it a draw."

Bolton had reloaded and now he started to drift to his right in an attempt to line up the last two bottles. When he thought he had it he raised the gun and fired, missing both bottles cleanly.

"I lose," he said. His arm dropped as if the gun weighed a ton.

Clint walked over to him and slapped him on the back.

"You owe me a gun, friend."

Bolton handed Clint back his weapon.

"Well, at least you'll have to come back here to pick it up," he said. He was still shaking his head at the incredible shot Clint had made.

"I'm going to go inside and pack my gear, Mick," Clint said. "It's time for me to get going."

"I think Mr. Dain is gonna be very happy with his new gun, Clint."

"I hope you're right, Mick," Clint said. "I hope you're right."

TWENTY

Vic Lennon didn't think things would progress this quickly. He had seen the old man leave that morning in a buggy, and the next thing he knew one of the men was telling him he was wanted at the house. When he got there Gloria Dain let him in. She was wearing a dress that was cut low in front to show just a little cleavage, and she smelled of some heady perfume he had never smelled before.

"You called for me, Mrs. Dain?" he asked.

They were standing in the entry hall of the house.

"Yes, Vic," she said. "I can call you Vic, can't I?"

"You're the boss's wife, ma'am," Lennon said. "I reckon you can call me anything you want."

"Well, I'm not talking to you now as the boss's wife, Vic."

"No?"

"No. Come inside with me, will you?"

He followed her into the living room, aware that

several of the men had seen him enter the house. It didn't seem to bother her, though, so he didn't think about it much either.

"Would you like some brandy?" she asked.

"Sure."

He'd had brandy once before and hadn't really liked it, but he was willing to drink with her because he knew where this was heading. He could *smell* it on her.

Gloria Dain, on the other hand, was thinking of the best way to go about seducing Vic Lennon. Was he going to be hard or easy? Already she was excited by the prospect of taking him to her bed—her husband's bed. She knew that Lawrence Dain wouldn't be back until tomorrow.

As she poured the brandy she was acutely aware that her nipples were hard. Also, she was wet between her legs. She wondered if, like some men, Lennon would be able to sense this, or smell it.

She turned and took a brandy to him.

"Thanks."

He was still standing.

"Sit down, please."

He looked around for a place to sit. She sat on the sofa and said, "Here, by me."

He sat next to her.

"How long do we play this game, Mrs. Dain?"

"Gloria," she said. "Call me Gloria."

"All right, Gloria," Lennon said. He set the glass of brandy down on a nearby table, untouched.

"What game are you referring to, Vic?"

"Put your brandy down," he said.

"Why?"

"Because you don't want to get it all over the sofa."

She stared at him for a moment and realized that he wasn't going to be so hard to seduce after all. She turned, put the brandy down, and then turned back.

He reached out and hooked his fingers into the front of her dress. As he pulled her to him, he was aware of how warm it was between her full breasts.

She came to him willingly, her open mouth meeting his. Their tongues mashed together, as did their bodies. Lennon exerted more pressure and the front of her dress tore. Her naked breasts bobbed free, and he took them in his hands and lifted them to his mouth.

"Yes," she said, "oh, yes . . ."

He licked and sucked her breasts, then pulled away from her so he could look at her. Her eyes were flashing, her naked breasts heaving, her nostrils flaring. He reached for her and tore the dress again and again until she was completely naked. He pushed her down onto the sofa and got down between her legs, where she was wet and waiting. He attacked her first with his mouth, licking her thighs and savoring the taste of her nectar, then plunging his tongue into her so that she gasped and lifted herself up off the sofa. He slid his hands beneath her and held her there so he could get at her better. He used his mouth and tongue on her until she was beating on his shoulders, wanting him to stop but not wanting him to stop . . .

Later they moved upstairs to the bed, where they were now. She was lying in the crook of his arm, her head on his shoulder. His other hand was behind his head and he was looking around the room.

"What would you do, Vic," she asked, "if my husband walked in here right now?"

"I thought you said he was going to be away until tomorrow."

"He is," she said. "I just want to know what you would do."

Without further hesitation he said, "I'd kill him."

She laughed.

"Del would jump out the window."

"I know."

She raked his chest with her nails and said, "This is what I've been missing, a real man."

"And what do you want from this real man, honey?" he asked.

"What makes you think I want anything more than what you just gave me?"

"I know you been workin' Del for weeks tryin' to get him to do somethin' for you."

"Like what?"

"Come on, Gloria," Lennon said, "who do you think told Del to agree to rob the Gunsmith for you?"

"I knew somebody was behind that," she said, playing with the hair on his chest.

"Not somebody," he said. "Me."

"And were you going to help him?"

"Sure," he said, "for a price."

"And will you help me now?"

"Sure," he said, and then added again, "for a price."

"You mean something more than I just gave you?" she asked.

"Baby," he said, "what you just gave me was great, but yeah, to rob the Gunsmith I'm gonna need a lot more incentive."

"We're talking about money?"

"Yeah, we're talking about money."

"Well," she said, "there's plenty of money, Vic."

"That's good."

"And there's plenty of me," she added, "that is, unless all you want is money."

"Honey," he said, "each one of you alone is great, but you and the money? That's a combination that can't be beat."

"You know, Vic," she said, "if you do this for me, there's a way that there can be a lot more money."

"We're talkin' now about killin' your husband."

"I never said that."

"You don't have to."

She hesitated, then asked, sliding her hand down between his legs, "And you'd do that? For me?"

"No, Gloria," he said, sliding one finger along the crease between her buttocks, "I'd do it for me."

TWENTY-ONE

When Clint rode into Rogue's Walk, Montana, he was surprised at the size of it. He knew nothing about the town, and consequently he hadn't expected much. Riding down the main street, though, he saw that it was a thriving community and, judging by the number of buildings that were being repaired or built, a growing one.

He stopped only to ask directions to the livery, where he left Duke in the hands of the liveryman with specific instructions on how to take care of him. The man listened, nodded, and told Clint not to worry. Clint took his saddlebags and rifle and went in search of a hotel.

He had decided to leave his team and rig in New Mexico, with Mick Bolton. He was, after all, going to have to return to pick up the new gun Bolton was making for him. In one of the saddlebags was Lawrence Dain's new gun, wrapped in cheesecloth.

He got himself a room in the first hotel he came to, although it wasn't the one he'd noticed when he'd ridden in. That had been the Rogue's Walk Hotel. This one just had the word HOTEL above the door, and while it wasn't as big or fancy as the other, it suited him just fine.

From the window of his hotel he studied the street. It was coming on toward dinnertime, so he figured he'd have something to eat and relax until the next morning. He'd sent a telegram announcing his early arrival date, but he'd managed to make it a day earlier than even that. Lawrence Dain and Henry Bollinger wouldn't be looking for him until tomorrow.

He used the pitcher and basin in the room to wash up from his ride, and then left in search of a likely piece of steak and some strong, black coffee.

It had been three weeks since Vic Lennon and Gloria Dain had become lovers and partners. During that time, though, they had managed to conceal the former from Del Nolan, who still thought he was Gloria's lover, even though they'd only been to bed a few times.

"Do you mind if I still sleep with him?" Gloria had asked Lennon.

"Hell, yes, I mind, but you got to keep him on a string. Hell, I mind if you sleep with your husband."

"Well," she said, "that only happens once or twice a week now."

"That's once or twice too many," Lennon said.

Something had happened that neither Gloria Dain

nor Vic Lennon had expected. The two had actually fallen in love. Lennon was the man Gloria had been looking for all her life. All she needed to do was combine the man with her husband's money.

Lennon had been waiting so long for Gloria that he'd been afraid when he finally got her—and he'd had no doubt that he would—he might lose interest. That had been his pattern with women, to lose interest after getting them into bed. This was not the case with Gloria, however. If anything, his interest was becoming stronger and stronger.

They had already modified their plan for robbing Clint Adams of the gun he'd made for Lawrence Dain. Lennon had brought two other men into the play, and one of them was standing across the street from the hotel when Clint Adams arrived. The other man had been waiting at the second hotel, so that they'd have both hotels covered.

The first man, Howie Engel, now ran to the second hotel to tell the other man, Ken Hall, that Adams had arrived.

"You sure it's him?"

"He fits the description."

"Let's check."

They went back to the hotel, and while Engel distracted the desk man Hall checked the register. He nodded to Engel when he had the information he needed and the two men left.

"It's him, all right," Hall said. "You keep watching and I'll ride out and tell Lennon that he's here."

"Gotcha."

• • •

Moments after Hall left, Engel saw Clint Adams leave the hotel. Nervously, he followed. If Adams noticed him and braced him, he had neither the skill nor the nerve to stand up to him. He was being paid enough to watch the man, and even follow him, but not nearly enough to face him.

He would need a hell of a lot more money to do that.

Clint saw the man as soon as he left the hotel. He'd been followed before, for various reasons. The most common was out of curiosity, usually somebody who recognized him and became fascinated with him. The second most common reason was because somebody recognized him and took it into his head to try him out. A lot of times he'd been able to talk the man out of it—or the boy, as the case was sometimes. He'd been followed for other reasons, but these were the most frequent. The first was usually harmless, the second—if talking didn't do the trick—often resulted in somebody getting killed.

He wondered what would happen in this instance.

TWENTY-TWO

Clint went to the nearest saloon, allowing the man to follow him. As long as the fellow didn't make any sudden moves, he was satisfied to know where he was.

He went to the saloon for two reasons. First, he wanted a beer. Second, the bartender would probably be able to tell him where to go for a meal and good coffee.

He entered and walked to the bar. His shadow did not follow him inside but chose to wait outside. That suited him, too.

"Help ya?"

He looked up to see the bartender staring at him with muddy brown eyes.

"Beer."

"Comin' up."

When the bartender set the frosty mug of beer in

front of him, Clint said, "Maybe you can help me with something else."

"Sure."

The man waited patiently while Clint took a healthy pull on the beer.

"A meal, and some good coffee."

"Just got into town, huh?"

"That's right.

"Partial to steak?"

"Good steak."

"The best in town," the man said. "When you leave here walk three blocks and then turn right. It's the first doorway on your right. You can't miss it."

"You related to the owner?"

"No," the man said, "I eat there, myself."

"That's a good recommendation," Clint said. "How's the coffee?"

"How do you like it?"

"Strong and black."

"It'll suit you."

"Thanks for the advice."

"Sure."

"Another question?"

"It's early," the man said, with a shrug. "I got the time."

"Who's the sheriff here?"

"Fella named Henry Jones," the bartender said, "but nobody calls him Henry. He don't like it. It makes him kinda mad."

"Hank?"

"Not that either."

"What do folks call him?"

"To his face, Sheriff Jones."

"And behind his back?"

"Partial."

"Pardon?"

"No, Partial."

"No," Clint said, "I meant pardon me, I didn't understand you."

" 'Partial' Jones," the bartender said. "That's what folks call him behind his back."

"Why?"

"'Cause that's a favorite word of his. He says he ain't 'partial' to being called Henry, and he is 'partial' to good whiskey. Like that."

"Partial Jones."

"That's right."

"I'll remember that."

"You a bounty hunter?"

"No," Clint said, "why do you ask me that?"

The man shrugged.

"Only fellas who ask for the sheriff when they first get to town are bounty hunters and lawmen. You don't look like a lawman."

Clint didn't know how to react to being told that he looked more like a bounty hunter than a lawman. Did you say thanks for something like that?

"I'm neither," Clint said. "I'm just the nosy type."

"Well," the bartender said, "would you also be nosy enough to want to know where the sheriff's office is?"

"Yes," Clint said, after another swallow of beer, "I would."

"I thought you might."

The bartender was in his early thirties, but apparently he'd had enough time behind the bar to know when a man had a reason for wanting a lawman that he didn't want to talk about.

"Well, his office is in the direction you're goin', but you'll have to go another block and cross over."

"Thanks."

"Sure. Anythin' else?"

"No," Clint said, "I think I'll just finish my beer."

He did so facing the room, his back to the bar. It was a small saloon, no gaming tables, just tables and chairs. It seemed the type of place men came to for serious drinking. There were no women working the floor, but like the bartender had said, it was still early.

He looked toward the front door and windows but couldn't see anything. His guess was that the man following him had taken up a place across the street. It occurred to him to seek a back exit, but he decided against it. He might be better off letting the man follow him to the sheriff's office and then having the lawman identify him. He could also use it as an opportunity to check in with Sheriff "Partial" Jones and let the man know that he was in town.

TWENTY-THREE

The man followed him to the sheriff's office and found himself a doorway across the street. He was standing there when Clint entered Partial Jones's office.

"Can I help you?" the man seated behind the desk asked.

He was in his forties, dark-haired with a mustache and no beard. He was sitting back in his chair, totally relaxed—or he appeared to be. No one who wore a badge was relaxed when a stranger walked into his office. No, this man *looked* relaxed, but to Clint's practiced eye he could see that the man was ready for anything that might happen. It was in the eyes. While the body seemed calm, the eyes were alive and alert.

"Sheriff Jones?"

"That's me."

"My name is Clint Adams."

Jones nodded.

"I know the name. Just get into town?"

"A short time ago. I thought I'd come over here and introduce myself, let you know I was here."

Jones scratched his nose and nodded again.

"I appreciate that, Mr. Adams. It makes my job easier. I'm partial to makin' my job easier. Can I ask you what your business is here in town?"

"My business is actually not in town. I'm here to see Lawrence Dain."

"Oh?" Jones said. "He's a very prominent citizen of our little community here."

"I know that."

"You have business with Mr. Dain?"

"I do. I have a gun to deliver to him."

"A gun?" Jones asked. "To deliver, you say. I understand Mr. Dain is very partial to guns. Is this for his, uh, collection?"

"It is. I built it for him."

"I see. So you haven't delivered it yet?"

"I haven't had the chance. I've only had time to check into the hotel down the street, have a beer, and come over here. Now I'm in search of a good meal."

"Maybe I can help."

"The bartender in the saloon suggested a café."

"Then you don't need me."

"Well, I do, for one thing."

"What's that?"

"Somebody's following me."

Jones frowned.

"I'm sure this has happened to you before."

"Yes, it has, but I was wondering if maybe you'd recognize this particular man."

"Where is he?"

"Well, last I saw of him he was standing in a doorway right across the street."

Jones got to his feet and Clint saw that he was taller than he looked when he was seated, probably a couple of inches over six feet. Most of his height seemed to be in his legs, which were very long. He crossed the room with an easy grace and joined Clint at the window.

"Where?"

"Right out there."

They both looked out the window together. There were people walking on the street, but there wasn't anyone loitering in a doorway.

"I don't see anyone," the sheriff said.

"Well, he *was* there."

"He isn't there now," Jones said. He looked at Clint. "What did he look like?"

"Sort of average. I never really got a good look at him. He's wearing a worn Walker Colt that might blow up in his hand one of these days."

Jones smiled.

"You didn't notice the man, but you noticed the gun, huh?"

"Occupational hazard, guns," Clint said. "I like to know if a man has a reliable weapon on him. This man's gun didn't look it." Clint noticed that the sheriff's own Colt was clean and had recently been oiled.

"So you're not worried about him."

"My feeling is he's keeping his eye on me for someone."

"Who?"

"That I don't know."

"Dain?"

"Maybe, but why?"

Jones shrugged.

"No, this fella is working for somebody else."

"I'll take a turn around town and see what I can see," Jones said. "In fact, I'll leave just after you. If somebody is followin' you I'll see him."

"Thanks."

"It's my job," Jones said. "I'm not partial to people botherin' visitors."

"I appreciate it, anyway."

"When will you be seein' Mr. Dain?"

"I think I'll be seeing his lawyer, Henry Bollinger, first."

"His office is just up the street," Jones said. "His name's on the window. You can't miss it."

"I'll stop in and see him tomorrow," Clint said. "He doesn't strike me as the kind of man I'd like to eat dinner with."

"I can understand that," Jones said. "The conversation would tend to put you to sleep. I'm partial to people who are a little more interestin'."

"Well, I think I'll go and hunt up that steak," Clint said. "Thanks for your help, Sheriff."

"Thanks for comin' in to see me, Mr. Adams."

Clint nodded and left. He stopped just outside the door to study the street, but the man who had been following him was apparently gone. Maybe he was scared off by the fact that Clint had gone into the sheriff's office. Since the man *was* gone Clint decided to stop thinking about him for the moment and concentrate on getting himself fed. He was starving!

TWENTY-FOUR

When Ken Hall rode up to the Dain house, Vic Lennon spotted him right away and started walking toward the stable. Hall saw him and altered his course from the house to the stable. Lennon was waiting for him when he dismounted.

"Adams is in town."

"Are you sure?"

Hall nodded.

"We checked the hotel register."

"Where's Engel?"

"He's keepin' an eye on him."

Lennon cursed.

"You should have kept an eye on him and sent Engel back here. Adams is going to spot him."

"Engel won't do nothin', Vic."

"I know that," Lennon said. "When I make my move against Adams, you're the one I'm relying on to back me up."

"And I will."

"Yeah, if Engel doesn't blow the whole deal by gettin' spotted first thing."

"Uh, Vic, you still ain't told me what this deal is," Hall complained.

"It's a lot of money in your pocket, Ken, that's all you need to know for now."

The promise of money was enough to satisfy Hall.

"So what do we do now?"

"We wait," Lennon said.

"For what?"

"The right time."

"And what do we do until then?"

"You go back to town and tell Engel I don't want him anywhere near Adams."

"You want me to keep an eye on him?"

"There's no point," Lennon said. "He just got here, he ain't about to leave. And we know what his next move is gonna be."

"What?"

"He'll go to see Bollinger, the old man's lawyer, and then he'll come out here."

"Today?"

"No," Lennon said, rubbing his jaw. "He'll probably see the lawyer tomorrow, and then Dain the next day."

"Why not tomorrow?"

"Naw," Lennon said, "a busy man like Dain will make Adams wait. We got until at least day after tomorrow."

"To do what?"

"Never mind," Lennon said. "Just get to town and

keep Engel where Adams can't see him. I'll be in later."

"Okay," Hall said. "You're the boss."

Lennon watched Hall ride away, then started for the house. He had to talk to Gloria first, and then to Del Nolan.

Gloria Dain opened the back door and saw Lennon standing there. She was surprised at her feelings. She'd been with him yesterday but had to spend the night with her husband. Now all she wanted to do was pull Lennon inside and make love to him on the kitchen table. That would have been difficult with her husband home.

She had told Lennon that any time he wanted to see her he could come to the back door and knock. Her husband never answered the back door. In fact, he never answered any of the doors in the house. They had a black manservant to do that. The cook usually answered the back door, but lately Gloria had been doing it.

"He's here," Lennon said.

"Adams?"

He nodded.

"He's in town."

"We have to act fast, Vic," she said urgently. She looked around, then stepped outside with him. He breathed in the smell of her and had to keep from taking her and crushing her to him.

"I don't want that gun getting to Lawrence."

"Relax," he said, and told her the same timetable he'd explained to Hall.

"I think you're right," she said when he was done. "Lawrence will make him wait."

"I'm going into town tonight," Lennon said.

"Will you do anything tonight?"

"I'll take Nolan with me, let people see him. Maybe I'll even let Adams see him."

"Don't let Del suspect anything," she said.

"Don't worry," Lennon said, "as far as he's concerned he's in charge, he recruited me."

"Well, be careful," she said. "Don't let Adams see you."

"I won't."

"And don't do anything foolish," she said, touching his arm. "Don't go getting yourself killed."

"I don't intend to," Lennon said. "I've still got a lot of living to do."

"And we'll have a lot of money to spend," she said. "You did mean that *we* have a lot of living to do, didn't you, Vic?"

"That's right," Lennon said. "That's what I meant."

She gave him a look and said, "You're going to have to stop thinking of yourself alone, Vic, and start thinking of us as . . . us."

He smiled and said, "I already have, Gloria."

TWENTY-FIVE

When Vic Lennon told Del Nolan that Clint Adams was in town the younger man's reaction was predictable. First, he was eager to ride into town and face Adams.

"I'm not afraid of him," he insisted.

His second reaction was caution.

"After all," he said, "he does have a reputation."

His third reaction was inactivity.

"Maybe we should just . . . wait."

"You can't wait on a woman like Gloria Dain, can you, Del?" Lennon asked. "I mean, if you want her, you got to do what she wants, right?"

"Well, yeah," Nolan said, "I guess . . . but . . ."

"But nothing," Lennon said. "I think we should ride into town and have a look at Mr. Clint Adams, Del. Whataya say?"

"Well . . . okay."

"Then let's get saddled up."

"You're goin' with me?"

"Well, sure," Lennon said. "I said *we* have to take a look. We're in this together, Del."

"Thanks, Vic," Nolan said. "You're a good friend."

Lennon had never had a good friend. He didn't know what it meant to have one, or be one, so he felt no guilt when Nolan made this remark.

Clint enjoyed his dinner immensely. Often he found that the food at the smaller cafés—rather than large restaurants or hotel dining rooms—was the best, and that was the case with this place. The steak was cooked to perfection, the vegetables almost melted in his mouth, and the coffee was—as the bartender promised—to his satisfaction.

"More coffee?" the waitress asked.

That was another thing that was interesting about the place. The waitress was a handsome woman in her thirties, with the strong, attractive hips and legs that went with her profession. She was the kind of woman he was preferring these days, experienced and full-bodied.

"Sure," he said, holding up his cup.

"You really like your coffee, don't you?"

"I live on it," he said.

"I made it."

"It's really good. Did you cook, too?"

"Oh, no," she said, standing there holding the coffeepot. There was a man and a woman at a table behind her, trying to attract her attention, but she didn't notice. "Not that I can't cook, mind you. I can, I just don't cook here. That's Lyle's job."

"Lyle."

"He's the cook, and the owner," she said. "He won't let anyone else cook. He's worried about the reputation of the place."

"Well, I can understand that."

"So can I," she said, then added wistfully, "but I wish he'd let me cook just once. I don't want to be a waitress all my life. I really am a very good cook."

"I'm sure you are."

The people behind her were starting to get frantic. They were starting to wave at Clint, but he chose to ignore them.

"You seem like a man who knows good food."

"I know what I like."

"Have you traveled a lot?"

"I've traveled a bit, yes."

"Ever been to New York?"

"Yes, I have."

"And San Francisco?"

"Yes," he said, "and Chicago, Denver, St. Louis, New Orleans . . ."

"Have you ever been to Europe?"

"I went to England once, also to South America, and Australia . . ."

"Let me cook for you."

"What?"

She sat down, putting the coffeepot on the table. The couple trying to get her attention gave up, got up and left.

"Let me cook you dinner," she said. "You'll be able to tell how good a cook I am."

"I'm not an expert—"

"But you've eaten in all those places," she said, "You know good food. My God, you've eaten in New Orleans. I can cook Creole food."

"Really?"

"And French."

It was starting to sound attractive—especially when he considered what else might happen. She had a very attractive mole at the right-hand corner of her upper lip.

"When would you want to do this?"

"Well . . . seein' as you've already eaten . . . how about tomorrow night?"

Clint thought for a moment, wondering if he'd still be out at Dain's then.

"I really am a good cook," she said, misunderstanding his hesitation.

"If I'm available tomorrow night it would be nice," he said, "but I have some business tomorrow and I don't know how long I'll be."

"What about the day after?"

"If I'm still here, I'd say yes."

She smiled, brightening her whole face.

"Good. Then it's settled."

"If I'm still here," he reminded her.

"All you have to do is let me know by that afternoon," she said.

"I will."

She stood up and looked around, suddenly aware that she had been ignoring the rest of the room.

"I better get back to work," she said. "Will I see you before then?"

"I'll probably eat here again," he said. "How is the breakfast here?"

"It's great," she said, "but mine's better."

She walked away before he could respond, which left him wondering if that was an opening she'd just given him.

He had already paid the bill prior to the last cup of coffee, so he stood up and left. He paused outside to look around, but there was still no sign of the man who had been following him earlier. He thought he might see the sheriff, but he wasn't around either.

He walked by Henry Bollinger's office, but as he expected it was closed. He decided to just spend the night around the town and stop in to see Bollinger in the morning.

TWENTY-SIX

It took Hall a while to find Howie Engel, and when he did it was in a small saloon at the south end of town.

"I've been lookin' all over for you," Hall said, joining Engel. "What the hell are you doin' here?"

"I'm drinkin'."

"I can see that, but I thought you were followin' Adams."

"I was, but he saw me."

"What?" That was just what Lennon had been afraid of. "Are you sure?"

Engel downed half a beer and wiped his mouth with the back of his hand.

"No, I ain't sure, but he went to the sheriff's office," Engel said. "Why would he do that if he didn't see me?"

"Lots of reasons," Hall said. "He's got a rep. He probably just wanted to check in with the local law, let them know he was around."

"Maybe . . ."

Hall noticed that Engel's hands were shaking.

"He didn't talk to you, did he?"

"Hell, no! I didn't go anywhere near him."

"Good, don't."

"I don't intend to," Engel said. "Did you tell Lennon he was here?"

"Yeah, I did."

"Did we get paid?"

"Not until the job is over."

"Well, what is the damn job?" Engel asked. "And why do we have to go up against the Gunsmith?"

"You don't have to go up against anybody," Hall said. "All you have to do is what you're told, and right now I'm tellin' you not to go anyplace where Adams might see you."

"Why not?"

"Because we don't want him to know anybody's interested in him."

"What if he already knows?"

"Maybe he doesn't," Hall said. "When he doesn't see you again, maybe he'll think he was imagining things."

"God, I hope so," Engel said. "I don't want him comin' after me." He looked at his partner. "Why don't we take on easier jobs?"

"Because easy jobs don't pay well, that's why, Howie," Hall said.

"You and your friends," Engel said.

"Lennon ain't my friend," Hall said, "he's just somebody I know."

"What's he doin' gettin' mixed up with somebody like Adams?"

"Apparently," Hall said, "whatever he's involved in means a lot of money."

"Any idea what it is?"

"No," Hall said, even though he did have an idea. He thought it had something to do with Gloria Dain, the beautiful wife of Lennon's employer. Lennon always did have an eye for the ladies, and they liked him.

"No," he said, "I have no idea." He waved at the bartender and said, "Can I get a beer, here?"

He looked at Engel.

"After this I've got to go and see Lennon. He's comin' to town."

"What about me?"

"Find a hole," Hall said, "and pull it in after you until I come and find you. All right?"

"That's fine with me," Engel said. "That suits me just fine."

The bartender put a beer in front of Hall, and he picked it up.

"Hey," Engel said, as if something had just occurred to him, "I'm still gonna get my share, right?"

Hall was startled, because he had just been thinking about that himself. Why should Engel get a full share for climbing into a hole and hiding?

"Don't worry, Howie," Ken Hall said, "you'll get what you deserve."

TWENTY-SEVEN

Clint found that the town had four saloons, including a small one at the south end of town that he didn't go in. The other two had gaming tables and girls and were packed, so he went back to the first one he'd gone to that afternoon to have a quiet beer after his walk around town. When he walked in he saw that the place was less than half full.

He'd been right in his initial impression that Rogue's Walk was a growing town. In walking around he saw many businesses and buildings that looked new, and others that were still being constructed.

"How was your dinner?" the bartender asked him.

"It was great," Clint said. "A good recommendation."

"Want to top it off with a beer?"

"That's why I came in."

The bartender brought him a beer.

"Been around town?"

"I took a look around."

"And you came back here? Most fellas would have gone to the Broken Wheel or the Rogue House."

Clint recognized the names of the two larger saloons.

"I get the feeling this was the first saloon in town," Clint said.

"Actually, it wasn't," the man said. "That was the White Horse, in the south end of town. In fact, in the beginning there was just that south end. All the rest of this has been built up over the past dozen or so years."

"And you own this place?"

"Yep, it's all mine," he said proudly. "The name's Jake Fellows."

"Clint Adams." They shook hands over the bar. If Fellows recognized the name, he gave no indication.

"My place has been here for the past ten years."

"I don't see a name outside."

"Had a sign for a while, but it got wore out, and one day some cowboys shot it down. It used to be called Jake's Saloon. Most folks nowadays just call it the Saloon."

"That's funny," Clint said. "The hotel I'm staying in has no sign outside either."

"Oh," Fellows said, "you're stayin' in my hotel?"

"You own that, too?"

"Yep," he said. "When I found this town I had no idea it was gonna grow this much. I opened a hotel and a saloon and thought I was gonna get rich."

"So what happened?"

"Other people found it, too, including Lawrence

Dain. When he started pouring money into it, the town it just started to grow."

"Well, maybe you're not rich, but you must be doing all right."

"I'm makin' a livin'," Fellows said, "but those other two places are takin' in all the money."

"And what about the White Horse?"

"I don't know how Dennis Mead is stayin' in business," Fellows said. "He owns the White Horse."

"Maybe you and he ought to get together and combine your businesses," Clint said.

"I don't think Dennis and me could be partners."

Just making conversation, Clint asked, "Well, who owns the other two places?"

"Well, the Broken Wheel is owned by a fella named Bundy, but the Rogue House is at least partly owned by Lawrence Dain."

"It is?" Clint was surprised.

Fellows nodded.

"The saloon, and the hotel that's attached to it. Do you know Dain?"

"No, I don't," Clint said, "but I've heard of him."

"Who hasn't?"

"Does he come to town often?"

"He don't," Fellows said, "but that wife of his does. Boy, is she pretty."

"I thought Dain was in his fifties?"

"He is, but his wife sure ain't. She's young and beautiful. Shows what you can get when you got money."

"I guess so."

"You want another beer?"

"Sure," Clint said, "why not?"

"I'll go and get it," Fellows said, "and then I'll tell you a little more about what goes on in this town."

TWENTY-EIGHT

Vic Lennon rode into town with Del Nolan, who was still acting nervous about meeting Clint Adams.

As they dismounted in front of the Rogue House Saloon, Nolan said, "I still don't know about this . . . seeing him, meeting him . . ."

"If you're gonna take a man on, Del, you've got to take his measure."

"I know, but—"

"You want Gloria, don't you?"

"Well, yes—"

"This is what she wants."

"I know, but I've been thinking . . ."

"About what?"

"About me and Gloria."

"What about you and Gloria?"

"Well, it's Mr. Dain . . ."

Lennon felt like he was pulling the words out of Nolan's mouth with his hands.

114

"Yes?"

"He's been real good to me ... making me foreman and all ... I feel bad about ... you know ..."

"You feel bad about him?"

"Yeah."

"What about her? What about Gloria? Don't you feel bad about her?"

"Well ... whataya mean?"

"About the way he treats her?"

"He ... he ignores her, I know that, except when he wants sex ..."

"He beats her, too."

"What?" Nolan looked shocked.

"She hasn't told you because she's afraid of what you'd do to him."

"H-how do you know?"

"A lot of the men know, Del," Lennon said. "It's you who doesn't know."

"That son of a bitch," Nolan said, color coming into his face.

"So you see," Lennon said, putting his arm around the younger man, "you've got to do this for her. It's her way out."

They entered the saloon and walked to the bar.

"Beer," Nolan said to the bartender.

"And whiskey, Paul," Lennon said to the man.

Nolan did not protest. Lennon knew he was going to have to get some liquor inside of Nolan tonight to get him to do what he wanted.

Clint worked on his second beer and listened to Fellows talk about the town.

"Lawrence Dain leaves big footprints in the streets here," he said, "and he hardly ever comes to town, unless it's to see his lawyer."

"Bollinger."

"Right. Sometimes he comes to town for a meeting of the town council, but even our mayor usually has to go out there to see him."

"That's what happens when you're an important man," Clint said. "Even politicians court you."

Fellows studied Clint for a few moments, then said, "I get the feeling you have business with Mr. Dain."

"You have good instincts."

"What's it about?"

"It's none of your business," Clint said, "but I'm here to deliver a gun for his collection."

"Ah," Fellows said, "so your business is his pleasure, huh?"

"I guess so."

"That man does like his guns, don't he?"

"That's what I hear," Clint said. "Have you ever met him?"

"Oh, sure," he said. "I'm on the council, so I see him when he comes to the meetings."

"What's he like?"

"He's like you'd expect a rich man to act," Fellows said. "He sits at the head of the table—where the mayor should sit—and acts like he's the king and we're the servants."

"And you all let him?"

Fellows leaned his elbows on the bar.

"Do you know what would happen to this town if

Dain moved away? Took all of his money out of the bank, out of the town?"

"Yes, I do," Clint said. "You might become a big man in this town."

Fellows thought that over and then stood up straight.

"You got a point there, friend."

"Clint."

"Clint . . . I guess that would make me a big fish in a little pond. Lots of people wouldn't want to live in a little pond, though. They'd probably leave town . . ."

"Making it an even smaller pond, huh?"

"Yeah."

They stood there quietly for a while.

"So I guess we put up with things the way they are, huh?"

"I guess so," Clint said, "unless you can find another rich man to take Dain's place."

"And he might turn out to be an even bigger son of a bitch than Lawrence Dain is."

"I once heard someone say that the devil you know is better than the devil you don't know."

Fellows took a moment and then brightened.

"I'm not real educated," he said, "but I understand that."

TWENTY-NINE

Hall found Lennon and Nolan in the Rogue House Saloon.

"Where's Adams?" Lennon asked.

"Uh . . . I don't know . . . exactly . . ."

"What do you mean, you don't know?"

"Well, I found Engel—"

"Jesus, he mucked it up, didn't he?"

"Well, he said he was following Adams and he thinks Adams saw him."

"Great."

"Adams went to the sheriff's office and Howie went and hid."

"That was the smartest thing he did. Is he sure Adams saw him?"

"No, he's not sure."

"Where is the idiot?"

"I told him to stay out of sight until I come looking for him."

"That was good. Where's he gonna be?"

"I don't know. I told him to find a hole and pull it in after him."

"Okay. Now all we need to do is locate Adams," Lennon said.

"That's right," Nolan said. "If we find out where he is, and he's not in his hotel, we can break into his room and get the gun."

"That's not—" Lennon started, and then he stopped.

"What gun?" Hall asked.

"Never mind," Lennon said. "That's a good idea, Del."

"It is?" Hall asked.

"It is?" Nolan asked.

"It is," Lennon said.

It wasn't what he had planned, but once Del Nolan said it he wondered why he hadn't thought of it before.

"We'll just steal the gun without him ever knowing we were there."

"That makes more sense to me," Nolan said. He obviously liked this idea better than facing Clint Adams.

"What gun?" Hall asked.

"Never mind," Lennon said. "I'll tell you about it later. Right now you go out and find out where Clint Adams is."

"How am I gonna do that?" Hall complained.

Lennon stared at him and said, "Where would you be on the first night you got into a new town, Ken?"

Hall thought a moment, then asked, "Where?"

"Check the saloons."

THIRTY

"Why don't you bring in some girls?" Clint asked Fellows.

They were still discussing his business, and Clint was suggesting ways to increase it.

"I'd have to pay them, wouldn't I?"

"Maybe they'd help you bring in the money to pay them with."

"If all I brought in was the money to pay them, why would I need them?"

"Why do I get the impression you like things just the way they are?"

"You know," Fellows said, "I didn't used to, but lately I been thinking how little pressure there is on me. I mean, when I first opened these places I thought I was gonna make money by the barrels. You know, I gave myself headaches tryin' to figure out what I was gonna do with all that money."

Clint scratched his head.

"I can see where that would give you a headache."

"Now this way I don't have to worry about money because I don't have any."

Clint looked around and saw that some of the men who had been there when he'd arrived had left.

"They went to the Rogue House or the Broken Wheel to gamble or get a girl."

"What about running a game in here?"

"What kind of game?"

"Roulette? Faro? Maybe poker."

"You play some poker, don't you?" Fellows asked.

That was the first hint that Fellows knew who he was. Part of Clint's reputation in recent years involved poker.

"I've been known to."

"You want a job?"

"Dealing?"

Fellows nodded.

"It did wonders in Tombstone when Wyatt Earp was dealin' faro."

Wonders for whom? Clint wondered. The whole situation in Tombstone exploded, and he was there to see.

"I don't think I'll be here that long, Jake," Clint said.

"That's okay," Fellows said, "I wouldn't have been able to pay you, anyway."

"You wouldn't have to pay anybody," Clint said. "Just hire a dealer and pay him a percentage."

"It's a thought," Fellows said, "but would I really be able to compete with the other two places? I don't think so."

"I guess not."

"Unless I had a dealer with a reputation."

"I don't hire out my reputation, Jake."

"Okay," Fellows said, "it was just a suggestion."

At that moment the batwing doors opened and Partial Jones entered.

"Here comes the law," Fellows said, loud enough for the sheriff to hear.

"Put a beer on the bar, Jake," Jones said, "or I'm closin' you down."

"Comin' up, Sheriff."

Jones joined Clint at the bar.

"Seen anybody followin' you lately, Mr. Adams?" he asked.

"Not since I saw you last, Sheriff."

"I watched you as you left my office and I didn't see anybody. Maybe you were wrong?"

"It's possible," Clint said, but he didn't think so.

Fellows came over and put a beer in front of Jones. Clint immediately got the feeling that the two men were good friends. It was the same kind of feeling he got when he was around Rick Hartman.

"Business is booming, I see," Jones said, looking around.

"We were just talkin' about ways of increasing business," Fellows said.

"Oh? What did you come up with?"

"Well, I tried to hire Clint, here, to deal poker for me, but he turned me down."

"Good," Jones said. He looked at Clint and said, "No offense, but that would cause more trouble for me than it would be worth."

"Don't worry, Sheriff," Clint said. "I won't change my mind."

"What's this about bein' followed?" Fellows asked both men.

Jones let Clint field the question.

"When I left here earlier I thought I saw somebody following me."

"Anybody I know?" Fellows asked.

"I didn't see him," Jones said.

Clint described the man to the bartender, who thought hard and then said, "Can't place 'im."

"Me neither," Jones said, "not from that description, anyway."

"Okay, okay," Clint said, "maybe he wasn't following me. Let's just forget it, for now. What brings you here, Sheriff?"

"Just makin' my rounds," Jones said. "I usually stop in here for a beer before and after."

Fellows had moved down the bar to serve another customer.

"I'm not partial to rushing my drinks," Jones told Clint. "You want to sit down?"

"Sure," Clint said. "I'm just killing time, anyway."

The two walked away from the bar and went to sit at a back table.

THIRTY-ONE

"Why are you doin' your drinkin' here?" Jones asked. "I thought you'd be at the Broken Wheel or the Rogue House."

"I like the way this place feels. What about you? How come you're not over there?"

"I'm not partial to Mead, so I don't go to the White Horse," Jones said, "and the other two places are just too damned noisy."

"Are you married?"

"No, why?"

"Just asking."

"You think I should be over at the Broken Wheel or the Rogue House looking for a girl?"

"I didn't say that."

"I take my job seriously, Mr. Adams," Jones said, "as I suspect you did when you wore a badge."

"That was a long time ago."

"Maybe, but I'm sure you took your badge seriously."

"I did."

That was the problem, Clint thought. Too many other people didn't take it seriously. He wondered how much things had changed for town sheriffs. Apparently not much, if they still had to deal with Lawrence Dain types.

"Well, I can't be seen in those places, or taking free . . . favors from those girls. So when I drink, I drink here."

"Also, you and Jake are friends."

"That's right," Jones said. "It shows, huh?"

"Yeah," Clint said, "it shows."

"Jake got here before me. When I came along Dain had just put up the Rogue House. A year later the Broken Wheel went up, and Jake's place has been like this ever since."

"I get the impression he likes it like this," Clint said.

"Yeah, he likes to give that impression," Jones said, "but once he had high hopes for this place, and for his hotel. I think those hopes died hard, and he doesn't want to leave any room for new ones."

"I'd help him if I could," Clint said.

"It's not your problem," Jones said. "Nobody's askin' you to help him. You'll do your business and ride out. There's nothin' wrong with that."

So why, Clint wondered, did he feel so bad?

Ken Hall found Clint Adams in Jake's Saloon, standing at the bar talking to Jake and the sheriff.

He stood outside, out of sight, and peered in through the front window.

He knew now how Howie Engel had felt when Adams went into the sheriff's office. It was a little unnerving to see the man talking to the law when you knew you were going to be . . . doing what? Hall still didn't know much about what Lennon had planned for Adams, except for something about stealing a gun. Wait, that made sense. Hall knew that Lawrence Dain collected guns, and he knew that Clint Adams was the Gunsmith. Obviously, the two were going to do some business together, something to do with a gun.

Hall had no way of knowing how long Clint Adams would be in the saloon, but he was there now, and that's what he had to tell Vic Lennon.

He left the window and hurried off to find Lennon and Nolan again.

"With the sheriff?" Del Nolan asked Hall.

"That's what I said."

"What are we gonna do, Vic?" Nolan asked. "Why is he talkin' to the sheriff?"

"I don't know, Del," Lennon said. "Maybe they're friends. Maybe they knew each other before Adams came to town."

"Yeah," Nolan said, "maybe . . ."

Hall had found them still at the Rogue House, standing at the bar.

"Look," Lennon said, "this was your idea, so you and I will go into Adams's room and find the gun."

"What about me?" Hall asked.

"You'll have to be the lookout."

"Why can't Engel do that?"

"Forget Engel," Lennon said. "Besides, you said yourself you don't know where he is. We can do this with just the three of us."

"Suits me," Hall said.

"Vic?" Nolan asked. "What if Adams comes back while we're in his room?"

"Ken will let us know, and we'll get out," Lennon said. "If we're gonna do this, Del, we got to do it now. Are you ready?"

Nolan took a deep breath. He had never stolen anything in his life, but there had never been a Gloria Dain in his life before. This was what she wanted done, and he was going to do it for her.

"Yeah, Vic," he said, "I guess I'm as ready as I'll ever be."

THIRTY-TWO

Clint sat and talked with the sheriff through two beers and then started to feel the fatigue from his trip.

"I think I'll turn in," he said.

"I've got to go and do the rest of my rounds, anyway," Jones said, as they both stood up. "I'm not partial to doin' them too late."

They left the saloon together, both waving at Jake Fellows, who waved back. Outside they split up and went in separate directions.

Clint walked to the hotel. When he entered the lobby he found it empty. The clerk was dozing behind his desk, his head down. Clint went up the stairs to the second floor and walked to his door. When he saw that it was ajar, he drew his gun and opened it slowly. The light from the hall was enough for him to see that the room was empty—almost.

He turned up the lamp on the wall and holstered

his gun. He turned the man on the floor over and saw that he had been stabbed to death. Clint didn't know him, had never seen him before, but here he was, dead in his room.

He looked around and saw that the room had been ransacked. His belongings were strewn about and the saddlebag where he had Dain's gun was empty.

Clint turned the lamp back down and left the room. He went down to the lobby to question the desk clerk to see if he had noticed anyone.

When he got downstairs he shook the desk clerk to wake him, but the man slid off his stool and fell to the floor. Clint went around behind the desk and saw that he, too, had been stabbed to death. Obviously, he had seen something, and it had gotten him killed.

"What's goin' on?" he heard a voice call.

He turned to the door and saw Sheriff Jones standing there.

"The desk clerk's dead," Clint said. "He was stabbed."

"Clem?"

Jones came forward and around the desk. He bent over the man and then stood up.

"What the hell happened here?" he demanded.

"I don't know," Clint said, "but there's more."

"Like what?"

"There's another dead man in my room," Clint said. "Stabbed, like this one."

"Who?"

"I don't know him. There's also something missing from my room."

"What?"

"The gun I came here to deliver to Lawrence Dain."

Jones looked down at the dead body, then back at Clint.

"Take me to your room."

Clint led the way upstairs, opened the door to his room, and turned the flame up on the lamp. Jones leaned over the body.

"Do you know him?"

"I do," Jones said, straightening up. "His name's Del Nolan. He's the foreman of the Dain ranch."

"The Dain ranch?" Clint asked. "This doesn't make sense. Somebody stole the gun I made for Dain. And killed this man. Why?"

"I don't know," Jones said, studying Clint. "I'm gonna ask you this once, Adams. Did you kill either one of these men?"

"No, I didn't."

"Do you have a knife?"

"I do."

"What kind?"

"A bowie," Clint said.

"Where is it?"

Clint didn't use it much, but he always kept it in a saddlebag. He went to the bag now and the knife wasn't there.

"It's not here. Somebody took that, too."

Jones stared at Clint.

"Sheriff, I didn't do it. I was with you at the saloon."

"You could have come back here and done it."

"I would have had to act pretty fast to clean myself up before you got here. This man put up a struggle."

His statement obviously made the sheriff stop and think.

"By the way, how did you happen to come over here? I thought you were doing your rounds in the other direction."

"I was, but a man came running over to me and told me something was wrong at the hotel."

"Who was it?"

"Nobody I ever saw before."

"What a coincidence that somebody should send you over here to find me with two bodies."

"Are you sayin' somebody tried to frame you?"

"That's exactly what I'm saying," Clint said. "I guess I wasn't imagining being followed, was I?"

"Maybe not . . . if you're tellin' the truth."

"I am."

Jones looked around the room, then back at Clint.

"Well, I've got no proof that you're lyin' so I'm not takin' you in, but don't plan on leavin' town."

"I'm not leaving town until I find that gun, Sheriff. That's a promise."

"I'll have you put in another room, and then I'll get this mess cleaned up. Jake's gonna spit when he hears about this."

He's not the only one spitting, Clint thought angrily.

"Why did you have to kill him?" Hall asked. "And the desk clerk?"

Lennon and Hall were riding back to the ranch in the dark.

"Nolan's my patsy, Ken," Lennon said, "he gets blamed for stealin' the gun, and Adams gets blamed for killin' him. The desk clerk saw us. He had to go."

"I don't like bein' involved in murder without bein' asked."

"So I didn't ask you," Lennon said. "You'll get paid a bonus for your trouble."

"What do we do about Adams, now?"

"Nothin'," Lennon said. "We just wait and see what the law does about him."

"Why would the sheriff do anything?"

"You told him there was trouble at the hotel, didn't you?"

"Like you told me."

"Well, he'll find Adams at the hotel with the two bodies. What would you think?"

"I guess I'd think he killed them."

"Well," Lennon said, "that's what we hope the sheriff thinks, too."

THIRTY-THREE

When Clint woke up the next morning he got dressed and went over to the sheriff's office. Partial Jones was sitting behind his desk.

"Find out anything about last night?" Clint asked.

"I questioned some people, but nobody saw anything. Anything else missing from your room?"

"No," Clint said, "just Dain's gun, and my knife."

"Well," Jones said, "I guess we can safely assume your knife did the killin', otherwise why take it."

"To frame me. They'll probably plant it somewhere you can find it."

"I'm not sayin' I believe you just yet, Clint," Jones said, "but that would make sense."

"You'll see."

"So who'd want to frame you?"

"That's a tough question, since I've never been here before."

"Does it have somethin' to do with Dain's gun?"

"Seems to."

"Somebody doesn't want him to get it. Why?"

"I intend to find out."

"Look, Clint," Jones said, "if you're innocent why don't you just stay out of it?"

"I put a lot of work into that gun, Sheriff."

"If it's the money, maybe Dain will pay you, anyway—" Jones started to say.

"It's not the money, Sheriff," Clint said. "Believe me, it's not the money. This is a personal matter now between me and whoever took the gun."

"Murder is my business, Clint."

"You find the murderer, then," Clint said, "and I'll find the man who stole that gun."

"They're probably one and the same."

"I know that."

"If it's not you."

"I don't think you believe that," Clint said.

Jones frowned and said, "Maybe I don't."

"How did Jake take the news?" Clint asked, changing the subject.

"Bad. Clem worked for him for a long time."

"Is he worried about business going bad?"

"He says it can't get much worse. He's only got you and three other guests in the place. Naw, he isn't worried about business."

Clint's stomach growled loudly and he said, "I've got to get some breakfast."

"Are you gonna see Dain today?"

"I don't know," Clint said. "I'll be seeing his lawyer, though, Bollinger."

"I wonder how Dain's gonna react to the news."

"I think it's safe to say he won't be happy."

"I'll be riding out there this morning to tell him about Nolan," Jones said. "He's gonna need a new foreman."

"I'll be around town, Sheriff. Like I said before, I'm not leaving until I find that gun."

"Just don't get between me and doin' my job, Clint," Partial Jones said, "and we'll do just fine."

"I don't think this is going to work, Vic," Gloria Dain said.

She was holding the new gun in her hand. They were in Del Nolan's empty foreman's shack.

"Why not?"

"You want everyone to think Clint Adams killed Del while he was stealing the gun, right?"

"That's right."

"So where's the gun?"

Lennon frowned.

"What do you mean?"

"I mean if Adams killed Del before he could steal the gun, why doesn't he have it?"

Lennon stood there for a moment thinking, then made a disgusted face and said, "Shit!"

THIRTY-FOUR

Clint walked to Henry Bollinger's office after breakfast at the café. The waitress had greeted him enthusiastically and he remembered two things. One, he had agreed to let her cook dinner for him if he was still in town the next day, and now it looked as if he would be. And two, he hadn't asked her name yesterday and hadn't given his.

"Really?" she said over his eggs. "You'll be here tomorrow?"

"And probably a few days after that," he said. "I have some unexpected business with the sheriff."

"You're not in trouble, are you?"

"I hope not."

"Well, at least you'll get a good home-cooked meal out of it."

Before he left the café he asked her name. It was

136

Ivy. He told her his name and promised to stop in and see her early tomorrow to confirm.

From the café he went to the lawyer's office. As the sheriff had said, it was easy to find because Bollinger's name was on the window. He entered and found himself in an empty outer office. Either Bollinger did not have a secretary, or it was her day off.

"Hello?" he called out. "Mr. Bollinger?"

He heard some movement in the other office and then Bollinger appeared at the door to the inner office.

"Oh, Mr. Adams. How nice to see you. Please, come inside."

Clint followed Bollinger into the office. The man sat behind his desk and looked at him expectantly.

"Where is it?"

"Mr. Bollinger, I have some bad news."

Bollinger frowned. Already he was wondering how he was going to break the news to Lawrence Dain, whatever it was.

"Didn't you finish the gun?"

"Oh, I finished it."

"And did you bring it with you?"

"I brought it with me."

"Then what's the problem?"

"It was stolen."

"What? Stolen?"

"Yes."

"When?"

"Last night."

"By whom."

"I don't know. It was stolen from my room."

"And you didn't see who it was?"

"I wasn't there."

"Why didn't you keep the gun with you?"

"It never occurred to me someone would want to steal it," Clint said. "It's only of value to Mr. Dain."

"What am I going to tell him?" Bollinger asked aloud, talking more to himself than to Clint.

"Uh, well, there's more."

"More?"

Clint nodded.

"There are two dead men involved."

"Oh, my—who?"

"The desk clerk in the hotel, a man named Clem."

"I don't know him. Who else?"

"A man named Del Nolan."

"Nolan?" Bollinger was shocked. "Del Nolan is dead? He was Mr. Dain's foreman."

"I know, the sheriff told me."

"How was he killed?"

"He was knifed, both he and the clerk. Nolan's body was found in my room."

"Wha—what's happening?"

"Well, I think someone wants to frame me for both murders."

"And the gun?"

"The gun's gone. That's where they made their mistake. If they wanted to frame me, they should have left the gun behind." Clint had thought about this over breakfast. "Then it would look like I killed Nolan while he was trying to rob my room."

"And now what?"

"Well, now we know someone was after the gun."

"How do I explain this to Mr. Dain?"

"You don't," Clint said. "The sheriff is going out there this morning to tell him."

"Oh." Bollinger looked relieved. "Well, I'll have to go out and talk to him, anyway, I suppose." Then softer, more to himself again, "At least I don't have to break the news to him."

"I would like to talk to him, too."

"About what? Oh, your money?"

"No, not the money," Clint said. "I just want the son of a bitch who stole the gun. I worked very hard on that weapon."

"Hmm? Oh, of course. Yes. I'm sure Mr. Dain will want to talk to you, as well."

"Good. Can we go out there today?"

"Hmm?" The man was still preoccupied. "Oh, I don't think so. He will be upset after he talks to the sheriff. He'll be in no mood to talk. Let me speak to him first . . . uh, later today. Perhaps in the morning I can take you out to see him."

Clint thought about arguing, but then decided otherwise. This would give him another twenty-four hours to look for the gun. Maybe by this time tomorrow morning he would have it back.

"How about I come back here at this time tomorrow?"

"Hmm? Oh, fine, yes, that's fine. This time tomorrow morning."

Clint left Bollinger's office wondering if the lawyer could have anything to do with the missing
gun.

THIRTY-FIVE

The day was suspenseful for Gloria Dain. First the sheriff came by to talk to her husband, and she wondered if anything would be said about her and Del Nolan. After all, somebody on the grounds must have known about them besides Vic Lennon. If Lennon was the only one, he certainly wouldn't have said anything. Still, she was nervous because she knew if Dain found out he would kick her out without a penny.

As usual, when her husband had a visitor in his office, she took up her position out in the hall so she could eavesdrop. . . .

Lawrence Dain stared at Sheriff Partial Jones across his desk, taking in what the man had just told him. A gun was missing, and two men were dead.

The first thing Dain said was, "My gun is gone?"

Two men dead, Jones thought, and all he can think about is his gun.

"Yes, sir, the gun and the lives of two men are gone," the lawman said.

"I understand that two men are dead, Sheriff. You think I'm coldhearted, I am not. Del Nolan was my foreman, and a fine young man, but I can't bring him back. I can, however, get my gun back. Where is Clint Adams?"

"He's in town. Why?"

"Is he suspected of these killings?"

"Let's just say I'm keeping an open mind on the subject."

"I would like to talk to Mr. Adams. Could you bring him here?"

"Mr. Dain," Jones said, "I'm not an errand boy—"

"Granted," Dain said. "Since you are going to town, Sheriff, would you mind informing Mr. Adams that I would like to see him, please?"

"I can do that," Jones said grudgingly.

"Thank you."

"What about your lawyer, Bollinger?"

"I suspect Henry will be out here very soon," Dain said. "By the way, I understand that you and Mr. Bollinger have the same first name."

"It's not a name I'm partial to, Mr. Dain."

"I'll keep that in mind, Sheriff."

Gloria hurried down the hall and hid in the living room as the sheriff left. It didn't sound as if the lawman truly suspected Clint Adams of the murders.

Lennon's plan was not working, but at least Gloria had the gun, which was the first step in her plan.

Jones actually passed Henry Bollinger on the road as he was riding back to town. Bollinger was riding in a fancy buggy.

"Have you informed Mr. Dain of what happened?" the lawyer asked.

"I did."

"How did he take it?"

"I'd say he took it real well," Jones said, "except for his gun. He wants to see Adams."

"I, uh, told Mr. Adams I would take him out to see Mr. Dain tomorrow."

"Well, Dain wants to see him today. He asked me to relay the message."

"I see. Well, since I'm already halfway there I'll just continue on."

"Good luck."

"Uh, yes, thank you."

Both men went their separate ways, Jones back to town, and Bollinger—nervously—on to the Dain ranch.

THIRTY-SIX

In Jake Fellows's saloon, Clint was commiserating with Fellows over the incidents that took place in his hotel the night before.

"I'm the one who should be apologizing to you, Clint," Fellows said. "You got robbed in my hotel."

"It's not your fault, Jake," Clint said. "Jesus, you lost a man last night."

"Well, I just hope the sheriff catches the son of a bitch who killed Clem, and poor Del Nolan."

"Well, at least you sound confident I didn't do it," Clint said. "That's more than I can say for the sheriff."

"Well, you *are* a stranger in town."

"I know, and he's just doing his job."

At that moment Sheriff Partial Jones walked into the saloon.

"Speak of the devil," Fellows said. "Beer or coffee?"

Jones saw that Clint had a mug of coffee in front of him.

"I'll have coffee, Jake."

"Comin' up."

"You're back from seeing Dain already?" Clint asked.

"He had only two things to say," Jones said.

"What were they?"

"Well, one was a comment about his gun."

"Nothing about the dead men?"

"He said they were gone and couldn't be brought back, but his gun could."

Fellows set a mug of coffee in front of Jones.

"What was the other thing?"

"He wanted to know where you were."

"He wants to see me?"

"That's right," Jones said, "and today."

"Bollinger said I wouldn't get in to see him until tomorrow."

"Bollinger was wrong," Jones said, "and he's probably getting an earful right now."

"Why didn't you bring Adams with you?" Lawrence Dain demanded of his attorney.

"I thought—"

"Sometimes, Henry, you think too damn much. You just should have brought him. Hopefully that idiot sheriff will deliver my message."

"Jones is no idiot—"

"If I say he's an idiot, then he is," Dain said, cutting the man off.

Bollinger didn't say anything.

"What happened last night?" Dain demanded. "What the hell was Del Nolan doing in town, getting killed in Clint Adams's room?"

"I don't know."

Dain was frowning.

"I suppose I have to name somebody foreman, but I can't think about that now."

"Somebody will have to run the ranch, Lawrence," Bollinger said.

"I know that," Dain said, gnawing on a fingernail, "but all I can think about is my gun." He looked at his lawyer and said, "You do it, Henry."

Aghast, Bollinger said, "I can't run a ranch, Lawrence."

"No, no, not run it," Dain said impatiently, "name a foreman."

"Me?"

"Yes, you," Dain said, getting up from his desk. "I'm going to go upstairs and lie down until Clint Adams gets here."

"If he gets here."

"He'll be here," Dain said. "He's going to want his money."

"When I spoke to him he said money was not the issue—" Bollinger started.

"Money is always an issue, Henry," Dain said. "You'd do well to remember that."

Bollinger watched as Lawrence Dain left the room. He thought that the meeting between his employer and Clint Adams was going to be very interesting indeed.

THIRTY-SEVEN

Gloria Dain met with Vic Lennon behind the livery stable. She relayed to him all the conversations she'd heard that morning in her husband's office.

"So Adams is comin' here today?"

"Sounds like it."

"I'll be on the lookout for him, then." He looked at Gloria and said, "I'm sorry, honey. I guess my plan didn't work."

"Don't worry about it, Vic," she said. "We've got the gun. If nothing else we can ransom it back to Lawrence. I'm sure he'd pay to get it back."

"You've got a lot more comin' than what he'd pay for that gun, Gloria."

"I know, but—"

"But nothin'," Lennon said. "Gunsmith or not,

we'll get what we've—what you have comin' to you."

"What are you going to do?" she asked.

"I have an idea," he said. "You better go on back to the house. Eventually Adams will arrive, and here's what I want you to do . . ."

"Be careful, Vic," she said when he finished his explanation. "Money is not going to do me any good without you."

"I'll be careful," he said. "You just do what I tell you and everything will work out."

As Gloria left the barn she thought that sounded like something every other man she ever knew had told her at one time or another in her life.

She didn't like hearing it.

Clint asked Sheriff Jones if he would go out to see Dain with him, but Jones declined.

"I saw enough of him for one day," the lawman said. "He's waitin' for you. You won't have any trouble gettin' in to see him."

Jones gave Clint directions on how to get there and wished him luck.

Clint went to the livery to reclaim Duke. If nothing else, the trip to the Dain ranch would give Duke a chance to stretch his legs.

Following the directions he soon came within sight of the Dain ranch. It was impressive. He didn't know the boundaries of the land, but the house was one of the largest he'd ever seen, two stories high and sprawling.

He rode toward the house, but before reaching it

he saw a man and a woman walking around behind the barn. The woman was a brunette, and although he couldn't see her face he knew she was beautiful. The man was tall and well built, but Clint couldn't see his face either. He continued to the house and was dismounting before he was challenged.

"Can I help ya?" a man asked.

"I'm here to see Mr. Dain."

"Is he expectin' ya?"

"Yes, he's expecting me."

"What's your name?"

"Clint Adams."

"I'll tell 'im."

Clint dropped Duke's reins to the ground, preferring that to tying him to a hitching post. He knew the big gelding wasn't going to go anywhere.

He waited patiently while the man went up the steps, knocked on the door, and was admitted. Moments later he came out and waved Clint to come up.

"This is Louis," the man said, indicating a black houseman. "He'll take you to Mr. Dain."

"Thank you."

Clint followed the white-haired black man down a hall to a doorway that led to an office. The walls were lined with books. Henry Bollinger was sitting in a chair in front of the desk, and a man—presumably Lawrence Dain—was seated behind it.

"Ah, Mr. Adams," Bollinger said, standing. "This is Mr. Lawrence Dain."

"Mr. Dain," Clint said, crossing the room.

Dain stood up and extended his hand. His grip was firm.

"Mr. Adams, it's a pleasure to meet you."

"And you, sir," Clint said. No matter what anyone had told him about Dain, he was determined to give the man a chance and form his own opinion of him. "I'm sorry it has to be under these circumstances," Clint said, releasing his hand.

"Yes," Dain said, "I understand there's been some trouble. Please, have a seat."

Clint sat down in a chair next to the lawyer.

"I've heard from the sheriff and Mr. Bollinger, here," Dain said, "now I would like to hear from you what happened."

"I'm afraid I know as much as they do, sir," Clint said. "Somebody broke into my room and stole the gun. There was also the body of a man—"

"Del Nolan," Dain said. "An employee of mine."

"Yes," Clint said, "he was found dead in my room. The desk clerk was also dead. Both were stabbed. I don't know if the deaths have any connection to the stolen gun."

"It seems likely to me," Dain said. "It would be too much of a coincidence to believe otherwise."

"I agree."

Dain stood up abruptly.

"Why don't we go into my gun room and talk? I can show you my collection at the same time."

"All right," Clint said, standing up.

Bollinger stood up, too, but Dain stopped him in his tracks.

"Not you, Henry," he said. "You can wait here."

"But I'd like to—"

"I want to talk to Mr. Adams alone," Dain said, cutting the man off. "You stay here and wait."

Bollinger looked like he wanted to argue, but in the end he sat back down in his chair to wait while Dain showed Clint down the hall to the gun room.

THIRTY-EIGHT

Clint followed Dain down the hall to a door he opened with a key. The room was a little bigger than the one they'd left the lawyer in, and the walls were lined with glass cases. Above the cases, on some of the walls, were mounted weapons.

"Impressive, isn't it?" Dain asked.

"Yes," Clint said, "very."

He spotted the Snaphaunce that was one of Dain's prizes, and the special case for the gun made for him by Sam Colt. He would have had more interest in the collection, though, if he were there under different circumstances.

"Mr. Dain," he said, "I'm sure you have a wonderful collection here, but I came to talk about the gun I made for you."

"Do you expect to be paid?"

"No, sir," Clint said, "not until I put the weapon in your hand."

"Do you think you have a chance of doing that?"

"I don't know," Clint said. "That's what I wanted to talk to you about."

"Me? How can I help you?"

"You can start by telling me who would steal the gun." Clint asked.

"Well," Dain said, looking not at Clint but at his collection, "that's easy."

"Is it?"

"Of course."

Clint waited, then asked impatiently, "Well . . . who?"

Dain turned and looked at him.

"Why, my wife, of course."

"You're saying your wife broke into my room and killed two men and stole the gun?"

"Well, of course she wouldn't do it herself."

"Then she'd hire it done?"

"Oh, no," Dain said, "she would probably have one of her lovers do it."

Clint didn't know what to say to that.

"Uh, how many lovers does she have, sir?"

"Well, at the moment I suspect she has one or two," Dain said. "That is, to be precise, she's probably down to one."

"How do you mean?"

"Del Nolan."

"Nolan was your wife's lover?"

"One of them," Dain said. "I'm sure she's behind the theft of the gun."

"You believe she had Nolan try to steal it?"

"I do."

"But he failed."

"Apparently."

"Then where's the gun?"

"He must have had an accomplice."

"Another lover?" Clint asked.

Dain smiled a humorless smile and said, "No doubt."

"Sir, don't you mind that your wife has lovers?" Clint asked.

"Not at all."

"Can I ask why?"

"I am at an age, Mr. Adams, where I do not require sex more than once or twice a week. My wife is young and beautiful and probably requires it more."

"And you don't mind if she gets it somewhere else?" Clint asked.

"As long as I get it when I want it," Dain said, "no, I don't mind."

Clint thought that was very . . . civilized.

"Does she know that you know?"

"I doubt it," Dain said. "My wife fancies herself a clever woman. She doesn't realize how out of her league she is when trying to match wits with me."

Clint thought about the woman he had seen by the barn as he rode up and felt sure this was Mrs. Gloria Dain. He wondered who the man with her was.

"Well, if this arrangement works, why would she want to have the gun stolen?"

"My wife believes I spend too much money on my . . . hobby, Mr. Adams—such as what I will be paying you when you finally deliver the gun to me."

"So you're confident that I'll manage to retrieve it?" Clint asked.

"A man of your reputation?" Dain asked. "Of course, especially now that you know where to look."

"Is your wife home right now, Mr. Dain?"

"I'm sure she's somewhere in the house," Dain said. "Please feel free to seek her out and question her."

"I just might do that," Clint said.

"And I will be right here," Dain said, with another humorless smile, "waiting."

THIRTY-NINE

Clint left the gun room and retraced his steps back to Dain's office. He wanted to stop there first and talk with the lawyer, Bollinger.

When he walked in, the man was sitting just as they'd left him.

"Where is Lawrence?"

"Still with his guns," Clint said. "I'd like to ask you a few questions, Mr. Bollinger."

"About what?"

"Not what," Clint said, "who. Gloria Dain."

"What about her?"

"Do you know that she's had affairs in the past?" Clint asked.

"Past and present, I imagine," Bollinger said. "Yes, I know."

"Del Nolan was one of her lovers."

"Was he?" Bollinger seemed surprised. "He's a little . . . young."

Clint saw something then. The lawyer was himself taken with the woman. He wondered if they had ever been lovers. Wouldn't Gloria Dain think that was funny?

"You didn't know about him?"

"No," Bollinger said. "Do you think she had anything to do with his death?"

"I don't know," Clint said. "What do you think?"

Bollinger looked taken aback.

"I don't think Gloria—uh, Mrs. Dain—would be capable of murder."

"Everybody is capable of murder."

"That's a cynical outlook."

"It's kept me alive this long."

"What do you plan to do?"

"I plan to talk to Mrs. Dain," Clint said. "Do you know of . . . any other lovers she has at the moment?"

"Uh, no, I'm afraid not."

Clint stared at the lawyer and asked, "You wouldn't happen to be one of her lovers, would you, Counselor?"

"Me? That's ridiculous! What could she possibly see in—"

"But you wish you were, don't you?"

Bollinger hesitated, then said, "She's a very beautiful woman."

"A brunette, right? Well built?"

"She's . . . very well formed."

"I think I saw her earlier today."

"Where?"

"Over near the barn. She was with a man."

"Who?"

"I don't know." Clint described him.

"That sounds like Vic Lennon."

"Who is Lennon?"

"Just a hand."

"*Just* a hand?"

"Well . . . he's always struck me as rather odd. Not your usual ranch hand."

"What's unusual about him?"

"Well, it's just a feeling . . ."

"That's okay, Counselor," Clint said. "I'm interested in your feelings. Go ahead."

"Well, I've always had the impression that he was . . . waiting."

"Waiting for what?"

"That's just it," Bollinger said. "I don't know."

"Vic Lennon."

"Yes."

"The name doesn't mean anything to me."

"Should it?"

Clint didn't answer. If Lennon was more than a ranch hand, he at least didn't have a reputation as a gun hand. If he did, Clint would know the name.

"Do you know where I can find Mrs. Dain right now?"

"No."

"I'll look through the house, then."

"How about the barn?"

"I'll look there next."

"What about Lennon?"

"I'll talk to him, too."

"What if he's the killer?"

"Then I'll find out."

"Shouldn't you tell the sheriff?"

"Sure, I'll tell him," Clint said, "after."

FORTY

Clint walked through the house. He saw the house-man and the cook and asked them both if they had seen Gloria Dain.

The cook was a hefty woman named Patricia who seemed to have something on her mind. She said she saw Mrs. Dain go out the back door a half hour earlier, maybe more. She had not yet returned.

Instead of going out the door to look for her, Clint asked a few more questions of the woman, hoping to draw her out.

"Would you happen to know where she went, Patricia?" he asked.

She didn't answer.

"Or who she's with?"

"Some man or other, I imagine," she said disapprovingly.

"Are you saying Mrs. Dain has lovers?"

"I shouldn't be talkin' about my employer." It was

clear that she *wanted* to talk, though.

"But Mrs. Dain is not your employer, Patricia," he said. "*Mr.* Dain is."

She hesitated, then said, "You have a point there."

"So?"

She turned and placed her hands on her ample hips.

"The fact is she steps out on Mr. Dain every chance she gets, with whoever is handy."

"And who is the lover of the moment?"

She frowned.

"It was Del Nolan for a while, wasn't it?"

"It was," she said, "but lately the man comin' to the back door has been that Vic Lennon."

"He comes right to the door?"

"Yes," she said, "he knocks and she answers. Then they go off together."

"And she does this in front of you?"

"I don't think she even sees me," she said.

"Why haven't you told Mr. Dain?"

"It would break his heart, that's why," she said. "I wouldn't hurt Mr. Dain for anything."

It was clear she was in love with her employer, but that was not a subject that concerned Clint. He didn't bother telling her that Dain already knew about his wife's infidelities.

"What do you know about Vic Lennon?"

"Nothin'," she said, turning her back, "and that's more than I care to."

Obviously, that was all he was going to get out of her, so he went to the back door and stepped out. He took two steps and then Gloria Dain came around from the side of the house. She was in a hurry and her head was down, so when she finally saw him she stopped with a startled cry.

Clint decided to go right on the offensive.

FORTY-ONE

"Where's Lennon?" he demanded.

"Who?"

"Vic Lennon," he said, "your lover."

"If my husband heard you talking like that he'd kill you."

"Your husband is the one who told me about your many lovers."

She frowned, unsure for a moment.

"That's a lie."

"No," Clint said, "it's not. He told me about all of your lovers."

"All?"

"Well, not their names," he said, "just that you've had many."

"Jesus," she said, looking astonished, "he knows about them?"

"Yes."

"Then why . . ."

"I guess he loves you."

That shut her up.

"Now, let's talk about the gun," Clint said, "and murder."

"I didn't murder anybody."

"Maybe not," Clint said, "but you knew about it."

"Not before," she said, "only after."

He was surprised that she wasn't denying it.

"How do you feel about one lover killing another one?" he asked.

"I don't know what you're talking about."

"Vic Lennon killed Del Nolan, didn't he?"

"I don't know."

"And what about the desk clerk in the hotel?"

"I don't know."

"Okay then," Clint said, "let's forget about that for now. The sheriff can deal with the killings. I want to know where the gun is."

"What gun?"

"The gun I made for your husband. The one you had your lover—whichever one—steal."

"I don't know what—"

"Oh, yes you do, Gloria. You know exactly what I'm talking about."

Seeing her up close Clint understood how she could get her lovers to do what she wanted, and why Lawrence Dain would put up with her infidelity. She was in her thirties, full-bodied, with silky black hair. In fact, he was strongly attracted to her himself, because she was exactly his type.

"I want that gun back."

"You just want to get paid."

"I don't care about the money," he said. "I put a lot of work into that gun and I don't want it in the hands of someone who can't appreciate it."

"You men and your guns," she said. "It's obscene to see him waste so much money on them."

"It's his money to waste."

"It's mine, too, now that I'm married to him."

"Discuss that with him," Clint said. "I just want the gun."

"I don't have it."

"Who does?"

Her eyes darted about like those of a cornered animal. He didn't know what her relationship with Vic Lennon was, beyond the obvious, but he sensed she was about to give him up.

"Vic has it."

"Where is he?"

"I don't know."

"I saw the two of you by the barn a little while ago, Gloria."

She bit her lip.

"Then maybe that's where he is."

"You better go inside and talk to your husband," Clint said. "Clear the air a little."

"What are you going to do?"

"I'm going to find Lennon and talk to him."

She looked down and said, "I guess you're right. I should talk to Lawrence."

She seemed contrite—too much so. He didn't envy Dain being married to her.

• • •

As Clint Adams walked away, Gloria Dain crossed her arms beneath her breasts. She'd go and talk to her husband, all right, but it wouldn't be to clear the air over anything. She wanted to know how a man could know about his wife cheating on him and put up with it, but she also wanted to have it out with him. She wanted to be free, and she wanted some money to take with her—a lot of money. Enough money to start over again somewhere else—with Vic Lennon, if he managed to survive an encounter with Clint Adams. Lennon satisfied her sexually more than any man she'd ever known, but she wasn't about to give up her share of the Dain fortune, even for him. If he was around to share it, fine. If not . . . well, she'd mourn, and then move on.

As Clint Adams rounded the corner of the house she turned and went into the kitchen. She was going to stop upstairs in her sewing room—where she kept things she didn't want her husband to see—and then find him and have it out.

Patricia, the cook, hunched her shoulders and ignored her as she passed through, then turned and frowned. Something was going on, and if it was something that was going to hurt Lawrence Dain, she wanted to know about it.

She left the kitchen, unaware of the fact that she was still carrying a large kitchen knife in her hand.

FORTY-TWO

Clint walked to the barn and entered. If Lennon had the gun, he intended to get it back today. As far as the murders were concerned, if Lennon had done them he'd turn him over to the sheriff.

The barn was empty, but as he turned to leave he stopped short. He lifted his chin and to anyone watching he might have resembled an animal testing the air with its snout. The fact was, he *sensed* danger, and felt that if he walked out the door now he'd probably run into a hail of bullets.

He looked around the barn for another way out, but there wasn't one. He had a sneaking suspicion that Gloria Dain had sent him right into a trap, and he'd taken the bait.

Now what?

In Rogue's Walk Partial Jones sat in his office, drumming his fingers on his desktop. He had the feeling that something was going on out at the Dain place, and if he stayed here much longer he was going to miss it. The missing gun, the murders, he felt that all the answers were out there.

He got to his feet, strapped on his gun, grabbed his hat, and left the office, heading for the livery stable.

Henry Bollinger sat in Lawrence Dain's office, wondering if he shouldn't be doing something else. With the gun being stolen and Del Nolan killed, it seemed fairly obvious that something was happening within the Dain household, but he still couldn't reconcile himself to the fact that Gloria might have had some men killed just to keep her husband from buying another gun.

He heard footsteps in the hallway and turned just in time to see Gloria enter the office. His heart leapt and he jumped to his feet.

"Gloria—"

"Where is he?"

"Uh, who?"

"Lawrence," she said. She had both hands behind her back, as if she was hiding something from him. "Where is he, Henry?"

"I, uh, believe he's still in his gun room."

"That figures," she said, shaking her head.

"Gloria, what—"

She didn't wait to hear what he had to say. She turned, still keeping whatever was in her hands out of his sight.

He wondered if he should follow. Moments later, he saw Patricia, the cook, pass the room. She never turned her head and probably didn't even know he was there.

Now he knew he had to follow, too, even if it was just out of curiosity.

"Where is he?" Hall complained.

"He's inside," Lennon said. "He can't get out without us seeing him."

"What about the other hands?" Hall asked. "What if someone comes—"

"They're all out doing their jobs, Ken," Lennon said. "We'll have enough time to do what we have to do."

"Are we gonna kill him?"

"We are."

"And then what?"

"And then," Lennon said, keeping his eyes on the barn doors, "you'll get paid. Now shut up and keep your eyes open."

FORTY-THREE

From inside the barn Clint called, "Lennon! Vic Lennon!"

Outside Ken Hall looked at Lennon in surprise.

"He knows we're out here, and he knows you. How?"

"I don't know."

"Mrs. Dain," Hall said. "She must have told him."

"Then why would he come here and go into the barn?" Lennon asked. "Besides, she wouldn't tell him."

"Well, he knows."

"A lot of good it's gonna do him."

"We should have brought Howie out here with us," Hall said. "Three guns would be better than two."

"Forget Engel," Lennon said. "He's out of it. It's just you and me, Ken, and a lot of money involved."

"Can't spend it if I'm dead," Hall complained.

"You're not gonna be dead," Lennon said, "he is."

"I hope so." Hall said.

Inside the barn Clint waited for an answer but one never came. If it was Lennon out there—and who else could it be?—he wasn't giving in. It was also likely that he had help. Clint had two options. He could run out, firing his own gun, and hope that when they shot at him they'd miss. Or he could look for another way out. There were no other doors, but there might be a window or some other way out.

He holstered his gun and moved further back into the barn. He didn't think it was likely they'd rush him at any moment, so he had some time to look the interior of the barn over.

A quick walk around told him that the barn was windowless. He'd have to look for another way. Most barns he had ever been in had a loose board somewhere in the wall. He started looking for a likely board. Once or twice he thought he found one, but when he touched it he'd find it to be firm. Whoever was in charge of the barn was keeping the structure good and sound.

No windows, no loose boards. He started to look for some tools that he might use to pry a board loose, but apparently they kept their tools in a different place. A spread this size would probably have a tool-shed.

There had to be some other way.

He walked to the door and called out again.

"Lennon! How long can we last this way?"

He knew the answer to that. He was the one
trapped inside. They were the ones with the advan-
tage.

They could just wait him out.

Or could they?

"Why don't you answer him?" Hall asked.

"I don't want to."

"But he knows it's you."

"He thinks it's me," Lennon said. "Why confirm it
for him? Let him wonder."

"You know, Vic, a man is a lot like an animal," Hall
said.

"What's that mean?"

"It means he's cornered. You know how mean a
cornered animal can be. Why, I cornered a squirrel
once, I was so hungry—"

"Ken."

"What?"

"Shut up."

Inside the barn Clint wondered how long it
would be before some of the other hands came
back. It was early in the day, and knowing the
way a ranch was run, the men had probably gone
out early for their day's work. That meant they
probably wouldn't be back for hours, maybe as
many as five or six. He certainly wouldn't starve
to death in that time, but there was another problem. While Lennon was keeping him pinned down
out here, what was happening inside the house?

It seemed pretty obvious that Gloria Dain had sent him into this trap.

What did she have planned for her own husband?

FORTY-FOUR

All Clint had at his disposal were horses. True, most of the horses were out with the ranch hands, but there were still a half a dozen or so in the barn. They were all he had, so he decided to use them.

First he put bridles on all of them, because he didn't want any of them to go running out of the barn too early. He wanted to be able to control them and send them all out at the same time.

Once they were all bridled, he toyed with the idea of putting a saddle on one of them. He could ride it out along with the other five, but he decided that Lennon might be looking for that. Once the first horse went out the door the man would probably expect Clint to be on one of them. If he simply ran out with the horses, or behind them, he could control Lennon and the man—or men—he had outside with him.

He walked toward the barn doors with the six animals behind him, then released the bridles and moved

174

around behind the horses. He couldn't yell to start them running, because that would tip off Lennon outside, so he slapped two of them hard on the rumps, stinging them and making them leap forward. The horses in front of them took the cue and started to run, and then so did Clint, drawing his gun.

"What the hell—" Hall said.

"Watch for him!" Lennon shouted, moving around from behind the corral door they were using as cover. "He'll be ridin' one of them."

The six horses came running out of the barn, with Lennon and Hall looking for Clint to be astride one of them. Because of that they did not see Clint running behind the horses until too late. They were out in the open when he fired, hitting Hall with his first shot. By the time Lennon realized what was going on it was too late. He tried to bring his gun to bear on Clint, but there just wasn't time. He squeezed the trigger anyway, by reflex. Clint fired and his bullet struck Vic Lennon in the chest. Lennon went to his knees, his gun pointed to the ground. He had time to empty the weapon into the dirt, his finger pulling the trigger convulsively—before he fell facedown in the dust.

The shots traveled and Sheriff Partial Jones, still a ways from the Dain spread, heard them and knew he had waited too long. The fuse had already run out. If he hurried, he might get there just in time to clean up the mess.

The shots were audible inside the house, as well, but the people there were beyond reacting to them. They had a drama all their own unfolding.

FORTY-FIVE

Gloria Dain found her husband mooning over his guns, as usual.

"You're a bastard," she said, without preamble.

He turned and looked at her, standing in the threshold of the room, then turned away. He spoke without looking at her.

"Is there a reason for that remark, my dear?"

"You knew," she said, "all along you knew and you didn't say anything."

"Knew," he said, as if mulling the word over. "Ah, I think I see. You mean I knew about your sordid little affairs with ranch hands? Oh, yes."

"They weren't all ranch hands," she said, and her defense sounded silly, even to her. "Why didn't you ever say anything?"

"Perhaps it was because it didn't matter, my dear. You performed your conjugal duties very well when called upon. That was all I ever required."

"You married me just to have sex with me twice a week?" she asked incredulously.

"Precisely."

"Then I was right," she said. "You are a bastard."

He heard a movement behind him and turned to see her pointing a gun at him. He stared at it in fascination.

"That's it, isn't it?" he asked. "That's my gun?"

"Yes, this is your damned gun," she said, holding it in both hands. "The gun you were going to pay so much money for."

"Let me see it."

"You can see it from there."

"Yes, I can," he said. "It's beautiful."

"It's going to kill you and all you can say is that it's beautiful?"

"Don't be silly, my dear," Dain said. "You're not going to kill me. Just give me the gun."

"You've been treating me as your own personal whore for the past three years. Why wouldn't I kill you?"

"Gloria, you have been treating yourself as a whore more often than I have," he said. "In fact, you were a whore when I met you. I never expected you to change."

"You son of a—"

"Instead of calling me names," he said, "why don't you tell me what you expected to gain by stealing my gun?"

"I just wanted you to feel the loss," she said. "And I didn't want you spending that amount of money on another silly gun."

"And what do you want now, Gloria? To kill me? Or do you want to leave me? With some money."

"I deserve it, for putting up with you for three years."

"Well then," he said, with a wave of his hand, "put a price on your annual services and I will pay it, but I want the gun."

As he said that he saw the cook, Patricia, appear in the doorway behind Gloria, who had taken several steps closer to him when she pointed the gun. In Patricia's hand was a kitchen knife. What was she going to do with that?

"I think I'll just kill you, Lawrence," Gloria said. "I think that would be better for everyone."

"No!" Patricia shouted, and rushed at Gloria with the knife.

Gloria, surprised and shocked by the voice, turned and accidently pulled the trigger, which she had been pressing very tightly against with her finger. The gun discharged, and a red hole blossomed on Patricia's chest. She staggered, dropped the knife, and then fell on top of it.

Henry Bollinger came into view then, staring down at the fallen woman—and the shots began outside.

"That must be Clint Adams, taking care of your . . . accomplice," Dain said to Gloria. "I think it's time for you to give me the gun, my dear."

Gloria Dain didn't know it, but she had just increased the value of the gun to him by taking a life with it.

Gloria was standing sideways now, trying to cover both Bollinger and her husband with it.

"Stay where you are, Henry," she said. "Don't make me shoot you."

Bollinger, certain that she would shoot him— hadn't she already killed someone?—held his hands up and said nothing.

"Gloria," Dain said, "give me my gun."

Gloria turned to almost face him and pointed the gun at him again.

"You're an evil man, Lawrence."

"No, I'm not," Dain said. "I want nothing more than to be left alone with my guns. What is evil about that?"

"It's evil the way you treat people," she said. "The way you treated me, the way you treat poor Henry . . ."

"Gloria, Gloria," Dain said, "you are the one who has killed someone, not I. And poor Patricia, who never did anything to you but serve your meals. What will you tell the sheriff about that?"

"That she came at me with a knife," Gloria said. "I had no choice."

"And I will testify that she was only trying to defend me."

"You'll be dead," Gloria said.

"Then pull the trigger, my dear," Lawrence Dain said, "because this is growing tiresome."

At that moment Bollinger heard something. He looked down the hall and saw Clint Adams coming toward him.

"Hurry!" he said.

His shout attracted Gloria's attention then, just as Clint came into view.

"Stay away!" she said nervously.

"Gloria," Clint said, "you can't shoot all of us, you know—and the sheriff is probably on his way out here." Clint didn't know that was true, he was just trying a bluff. He looked down at the fallen woman, wondering for a brief moment how she happened to get in the middle of this.

"He has to die," she said.

"No, he doesn't," Clint said. "If you want a lover, or you don't like the way he treats you, you have the right to leave, but you don't have the right to kill him."

"W-what happened to Vic?"

"Lennon is dead," Clint said, "and his friend with him. It's all over. He killed Nolan and the desk clerk, I bet, and you didn't know it until after it was over."

"T-that's right."

"And I don't know what happened here, but maybe it was an accident. If you kill him now, though, that's murder in cold blood. The counselor, here, and I are witnesses, and you won't be able to kill us, too. We'll get the gun from you before you can pull the trigger again. Then you'll go to prison. Is it worth it?"

She thought his words over.

"All he wants is his damn gun," she complained. "That's all he cares about."

"Then give it to him," Clint said, "and leave him, but don't ruin the rest of your life over it."

She hesitated, holding the gun nervously in both hands. Clint took a step toward her, then another, and kept coming until he was able to reach out and take the gun from her.

"Give me my gun," Dain said.

Clint ejected all of the shells from the gun, letting them fall to the floor, then tossed it to Dain.

"Here," Clint said. "I didn't know when I accepted the commission to build it that it would cause all this trouble."

"That's ridiculous," Dain said, holding the weapon lovingly in his hands. "The gun did not cause the trouble, people did."

"You especially," Clint said.

"Perhaps you're right," Dain said. "Perhaps you are."

He didn't seem too upset at the prospect, though. Clint heard a horse outside and went to the window. He saw the sheriff ride up and dismount, checking the bodies on the ground.

"The sheriff's here," Clint said. He turned to speak to Bollinger and Gloria. "Let's go out and explain everything to him."

EPILOGUE

Clint rolled over in bed and bumped into Ivy's hip. He reached out and ran his hand over it, enjoying the smoothness of her skin beneath his palm.

It was Friday morning now. Wednesday, after the trouble at the Dain ranch, Clint, Gloria and Lawrence Dain, and Henry Bollinger had spent the better part of the afternoon and evening talking to Sheriff Partial Jones. Jones had asked questions relentlessly until he had everything straight in his mind and then he had reluctantly put Gloria Dain in a cell to await the arrival of a judge.

Thursday Clint had talked with Dain about the money owed him . . .

"I don't want it."

"What?" Dain said from behind his desk. "Are you mad? You fulfilled your part of the bargain."

"I know I did," Clint said. "I'm not saying I don't

want payment, I just don't want the agreed upon amount."

"Ah." This was something Lawrence Dain could understand. "You want more."

"No."

"Then I don't understand."

"I want you to pay all of your wife's legal fees."

"For killing my cook and trying to kill me?"

"Exactly." Clint didn't bother arguing that Gloria had not actually tried to kill him. She did, however, kill the poor cook, and for that she'd have to stand trial.

"I want you to get her the best lawyer possible."

"I can have Henry—"

"I think being a witness would exclude Mr. Bollinger from defending her. No, I want you to hire some high-priced lawyer to defend her, or our deal is off and I'll take the gun back with me."

Dain did not even have to think about it. He agreed.

That evening Clint had gone to Ivy's rooms above the general store to let her cook him a meal. True to her word, she was an excellent cook and he had enjoyed the meal immensely. What he had enjoyed even more, however, was after the meal when she had let her dress fall to the floor, saying, "And now for dessert."

She had full hips and breasts, large brown, sensitive nipples. A woman in her thirties, she had some experience in bed, and was eager to please.

He ran his hand over her hip now, and around over

the cheeks of her marvelous ass. He had told her that he would be leaving in the morning no matter what. She had said she understood that and wasn't asking him for anything more than what he was willing to give.

Clint wished he'd never taken on the Dain commission. Maybe Dain was right, maybe it wasn't the gun that caused all of the trouble, but if not for the gun then he wouldn't have been there in the middle of it. He was anxious to put Rogue's Walk behind him.

Ivy awoke and turned over, smiling at him. He slid his hand up over her rounded belly to her breasts, caressing the nipples until they were hard.

"Time to leave?" she asked.

"Not quite," he said, "not just yet."

Watch for

THE ELLIOTT BAY MURDERS

170th in the exciting GUNSMITH series
from Jove

Coming in February!

If you enjoyed this book, subscribe now and get...

TWO FREE

A $7.00 VALUE–

If you would like to read more of the very best, most exciting, adventurous, action-packed Westerns being published today, you'll want to subscribe to True Value's Western Home Subscription Service.

Each month the editors of True Value will select the 6 very best Westerns from America's leading publishers for special readers like you. You'll be able to preview these new titles as soon as they are published, *FREE* for ten days with no obligation!

TWO FREE BOOKS

When you subscribe, we'll send you your first month's shipment of the newest and best 6 Westerns for you to preview. With your first shipment, two of these books will be yours as our introductory gift to you absolutely *FREE* (a $7.00 value), regardless of what you decide to do. If you like them, as much as we think you will, keep all six books but pay for just 4 at the low subscriber rate of just $2.75 each. If you decide to return them, keep 2 of the titles as our gift. No obligation.

Special Subscriber Savings

When you become a True Value subscriber you'll save money several ways. First, all regular monthly selections will be billed at the low subscriber price of just $2.75 each. That's at least a savings of $4.50 each month below the publishers price. Second, there is never any shipping, handling or other hidden charges—*Free home delivery*. What's more there is no minimum number of books you must buy, you may return any selection for full credit and you can cancel your subscription at any time. A TRUE VALUE!

A special offer for people who enjoy reading the best 'Westerns published today.

WESTERNS!

NO OBLIGATION

Mail the coupon below

To start your subscription and receive 2 FREE WESTERNS, fill out the coupon below and mail it today. We'll send your first shipment which includes 2 FREE BOOKS as soon as we receive it.